THE BRIGHT FACE OF DANGER

THE BRIGHT FACE OF DANGER

Roger Ormerod

Chivers Press   •   Thorndike Press
Bath, England   Waterville, Maine USA

LgPt Orm

This Large Print edition is published by Chivers Press, England, and by Thorndike Press, USA.

Published in 2002 in the U.K. by arrangement with the author c/o Juliet Burton Literary Agency.

Published in 2002 in the U.S. by arrangement with Juliet Burton Literary Agency.

U.K. Hardcover   ISBN 0–7540–7442–0 (Chivers Large Print)
U.K. Softcover   ISBN 0–7540–7443–9 (Camden Large Print)
U.S. Softcover   ISBN 0–7862–4543–3 (Nightingale Series Edition)

The text of this Large Print edition is unabridged.
Other aspects of the book may vary from the original edition.

Set in 16 pt. New Times Roman.

Printed in Great Britain on acid-free paper.

British Library Cataloguing in Publication Data available

Library of Congress Cataloging-in-Publication Data

Ormerod, Roger.
    The bright face of danger / Roger Ormerod.
       p. cm.
    ISBN 0–7862–4543–3 (lg. print : sc : alk. paper)
    1. Private investigators—England—Fiction. 2. Large type books.
    I. Title.
PR6065.R688 B74 2002
823'.914—dc21   2002075214

CHAPTER ONE

I shall always believe that I hounded him to his death. It's no good trying to convince myself that it was a normal interrogation, and there's no point in pleading that I did not understand what I was doing. I should have known. The evidence was there. Simply, I had failed to organise it in my mind.

All right, so there was some excuse. I was distracted. George—that's George Coe, my partner—had not been himself right from the beginning. Or perhaps he had been too much his normal self. That was something else I should have taken into consideration.

I assumed that George knew what we had taken on, but George reads only the sports pages. When he said: 'Dave, what the hell've you got us into?' it would perhaps have been better to explain the background, and allow him to walk away from it.

But George is inscrutable. During the whole of that initial interview I could read nothing in his expression. But after all, I was concentrating on Adrian Collis, with odd glances at his wife.

We had driven up on the Tuesday afternoon, the 7th February it would be, using my Porsche. George is never happy having to squeeze his bulk into the little car. We got out, he stiffly, to look at the bungalow. Collis had been released a week before.

Firbelow, he called it. I understand that being an architect he designed it himself, having acquired the plot of land and planning permission some years before. Some people have that sort of influence. The sprawled bungalow sat in about two acres of ground, seeming, from the road, to have a Spanish influence. There was a hint of an inner courtyard, a patio. Apart from the relief of one shallow gable-end, the roofing was flat. There was a lot of cedar cladding; the sloping roof was tiled with cedar shingles. All this was intended to harmonise with the surroundings, because the bungalow stood on the high rise to the east of the Chase, looking from its rear over the valley. The sun was lowering, the air crisp, with only a hint of mist developing in the far distance. Already the town lights were glowing blood red and blue, down there on the dark floor of the valley, like a ruby and amethyst necklace tossed away negligently.

The town! We had driven through it before sweeping on up the hill. It was a dour and friendless place, harsh in its planning and soulless in its concentricity. The streets flowed down to the centre like long sinuous spokes, lines of terraced houses marching up and down the slopes with no relief from nerveless conformity. Fifty years before, this had been a prosperous mining area. But the seams had

2

run out. It had left the town to live as it might, and still the strain of survival rested harshly on the community. They were not people who easily forgot or forgave. You could almost feel the enmity seeping up towards the bungalow, rising with the shadows in the valley like the mists above the trees.

George shivered. The car had been warm. We were standing at a five-barred gate painted white, the railing effect being carried on all the way round the perimeter of the site as a four foot high fence. Behind us the sky was purple-black. There were lights on in the bungalow, many lights, like a boy whistling in the dark. From somewhere behind the building came the deep, heart-catching baying of a large dog. I guessed a Great Dane. I think they call it its bell. A strange word; bells are supposed to beckon. I felt like turning and running as fast as I could.

We saw it burst round from the side, a shadow on which a window light briefly fell. He was moving with that long, effortless stride they have, occasionally lifting his head to warn us he was in no mood for discussion.

I said: 'Have you got any cheese, George?'

'Not on me.'

'All dogs love cheese. The smellier the better. Don't let him think you're scared.'

The dog could have taken the fence in his stride.

'He can smell I'm scared,' said George.

3

We waited. The dog came up to the gate and swerved himself to a halt, then put his rear end on the ground, curled his tail round, and sat grinning at us, saliva dripping from as nice a set of teeth as I've ever seen.

I think we were hypnotised. When Collis spoke, neither George nor I had noticed his approach.

'Who are you?'

He was standing with his back to the last of the light, his face shadowed. He was tall, with slim shoulders and a lot of fair hair that caught the fading red of the sunset. There was a shape under his arm that looked very like a shotgun.

'My name is David Mallin,' I said. 'And this is my partner, George Coe.'

'Identification?'

I slid my hand into a pocket to produce my wallet, and extracted one of our cards. Mallin & Coe—Confidential Enquiries.

His torch stabbed at my hand. He did not move closer; his eyes must have been keen.

'You'd better come in,' he said. 'Bring the car up the drive, or you're likely to get it damaged.'

'The dog . . .'

He laughed. 'He knows you're friends. I told him so.'

He was unlocking a huge padlock on the gate. George looked round desperately as I turned to the car. He was too late. The dog gave a yip of delight and bounded at him, put

4

two huge paws on his shoulders, and tried to lick the flesh from his face. Perhaps George's fear smelt of cheese.

I bubbled the car along quietly behind them as they walked up the straight drive. The plot had been landscaped no more than a year before. The lawn was immature, and there was no character in the layout. There was an air of neglect. They had planted a row of cypresses along the front, but they were barely six feet high. *Cupressus Leylandii*, I think, the fast-growing strain. But we couldn't wait for their protection.

To one side of the building there was a two-car garage with its doors up, and inside one large car and a smaller one. Beyond that, a car-port. I left the Porsche under its protection. Adrian Collis and George were standing in the entrance porch in front of the open front door. It was light oak, studded with square-headed nails. Collis was looking out across the road, where the massed conifers and silver birch stood like black lace against the slightly lighter sky.

'They'll be here in a little while,' he said softly. 'They come up the hill, leave their cars in the trees, and then they just lurk around, watching. Always watching. My dog, Major, patrols all night.'

Major! The dog panted at my elbow. He was grey and white; not military colours in this country.

'Is that safe?' I asked. 'He could be over that fence in a flash.'

There was a smile in his voice. 'He's a fully-trained guard dog. I had him from the best kennels in the country. You simply show him the boundaries, and leave it all to him.'

'I hope he knows them. How long has he been here?'

'Since Saturday. The Chief Warden was good enough to give me the address of the kennels. Major's been a great comfort. Isn't that so, dear?'

He turned quickly. I had not been aware of the woman standing just behind us in the hall.

She would have been a little under thirty, I thought, a trim, small woman with chestnut hair and those clear blue compelling eyes you sometimes get with that colouring. She had been silent, with the tight containment of patience. Her fingers were locked together in front of her. There was a nobleness to her brow and a quiet, comfortable dependence in her attitude.

'With Major here,' he said, 'there's absolutely nothing to be frightened of, is there Delia?'

She smiled, her lips moving into the prescribed shape. 'Nothing,' she said throatily. The blue eyes were vacant with fear.

'Send 'em off, boy,' he said gently, and he clicked his tongue with pleasure when the dog bounded away.

6

George met my gaze. He shook his head slightly, as though I had been about to say something. Behind us, Delia Collis slammed the door vigorously, and when I turned she was smoothing her skirt with her fingertips; or cleansing them perhaps.

The hall was square, wood-block tiled and highly polished. I avoided carefully the four small scarlet carpets. Four doors opened from the hall, and two corridors, the effect of soft and graded shadows being achieved by carefully-spaced wall lights. Collis led the way, as though he had invited us in for a drink and a listen to his hi-fi. Delia Collis, although I tried to dawdle, hung behind.

'The terms we discussed over the phone are acceptable,' Collis was saying. 'Of course, I couldn't afford to let it go on too long, but I don't anticipate it will.'

The room was magnificent. He had probably designed the whole building around this room, somehow managing to convey spaciousness without the emptiness that usually goes with it, yet achieving the effect without cramming it with furniture. What there was seemed to glow with light—sheeny oak and red coverings—a low three-seater settee against the back wall, two easy chairs and three not-so-easy ones. An end wall was completely devoted to the speakers and music centre, the racked discs and decked tapes of a comprehensive stereo system. Central above it was a single glowing painting of Notre Dame, softly in the distance between the sun-drenched, rain-soaked buildings of a Parisian street.

The one longest wall was a complete window. He touched a button, I think, and the curtains slid aside, and then he turned off the light switch. The moon had risen. The mist lay gently billowing beneath us, flooding the valley. In the far distance the opposite slopes, grey and brown and black with massed firs, were etched white where the moon caught the frost.

'I find I prefer it with the town obscured,' he said tonelessly.

Then the lights were on again and the curtains sliding shut. I looked at my feet. George cleared his throat. Delia spoke in a conversational voice, asking what we would like to drink.

I had lager, George a short whisky. We stood awkwardly, watching Collis prowling. Even Delia remained on her feet, her back against the stereo cupboard, which had proved to hide the bottles.

'It must be clear to you that I need protection,' Collis was saying. 'You've seen.' Actually, we had seen nothing threatening. He caught my expression and grimaced. 'But you will. Oh, I can assure you you will, before you leave.'

'We're leaving, then?' George said abruptly.

Something gave his voice a tone of challenge. But he seemed relaxed; the only one in the room. He was searching round for a chair large enough for his behind. 'We got the impression you want protection. Am I right? You've got a dog and a gun, but you want more. Me and Dave. Toughies, to guard the place. So what's this leaving business?'

It sounded ungracious, very unlike George. He sat, moving his free hand in a dismissive way. Collis walked towards him jerkily. He had an aquiline face, which he pushed forward as he moved, and long, elegant hands, white and clean, thrusting from snow-white cuffs. George looked up at him, his eyes wide, and cut in before Collis could speak.

'So what the hell *is* this?'

Collis stopped. He moved his hands apart in a small gesture of defeat. Strangely, Delia laughed, a flat sound with a catch to it.

'So you're not so famous, Adrian.'

I had been certain George would have known the name. I felt I should explain for him.

'George reads only the sports page.'

George looked at me. 'And the letters,' he murmured, hurt. I nodded placatingly. 'And the horoscopes.'

I sat down quickly where I could watch him, then looked round for Delia. She was circling the room, came to a halt behind George's chair, and stood with one hand on its back. She

9

approved of the great oaf, simply because of his ignorance. I saw amusement in George's eyes.

I said: 'Let me explain.' And Collis gave a gesture of mock defeat, turning away to allow me to get on with it. I supposed his stooped shoulders came from bending over a drawing board. I chose my words carefully, committing myself to nothing.

'A summary. I could have a fact or two wrong. Adrian Collis, arrested nine months ago for the rape and murder of three young women, eighteen, seventeen and twenty years old, in that order.'

'Madge Goldwater,' said Delia over George's head. Her eyes were dark. 'Little Tina, and Marilyn Partridge.'

'I hadn't memorised their names.'

'I knew Tina.'

'I'm sorry.'

'Not very well. She was a strange, startled sort of girl. I'd never managed to get more than a few words out of her . . .'

'Delia!'

She lifted her chin to him, then she relaxed. 'But do carry on, Mr. Mallin.'

'Three young women,' I carried on, avoiding George's eyes. 'Two single, the third married. All strangled within ten miles of here, one in December, I think, one about January—'

'Oh, for heaven's sake!' burst out Collis. I saw he had made himself a drink, but none for

10

Delia. 'If you don't know the facts . . .'

George rumbled. 'David was trying not to hurt your feelings.'

'Do you think I've got any left? Use your imagination, man. If you've stood in a box and listened to the whole sordid story being laid out in detail, felt the eyes on you, hating you, waited for the verdict . . . You can't afford feelings if you want to keep your sanity.'

I waited politely. High on his prominent cheekbones were twin patches of colour. Delia watched him with subdued concern. He was abruptly calm.

'Madge Goldwater,' he said, 'aged eighteen, killed on Tuesday the 4th January, last year. Tina Fletcher, not quite seventeen—Wednesday the 23rd February, and Marilyn Partridge, married two years, nearly twenty-one, on Wednesday the 18th May. Each one late in the evening, after dark, in a quiet stretch of the Chase. On each night I was late home. I'd been to see constructions in Peterborough and Stoke-on-Trent. That was confirmed. I had no alibis. There were car tracks very like my own, but I had new tyres and couldn't remember when, or prove it. The blood groups matched, but mine is not uncommon. The evidence was circumstantial —odd reported sightings of a car like mine, but none agreeing as to colour. It was pitiful.'

'The evidence?' asked George, dangerously polite.

'That,' agreed Collis, '. . . too.'

'Then they had a confession,' George suggested.

'They did not.'

George nodded at me knowingly. I tried not to respond.

'And what does *that* mean?' burst out Collis.

George shrugged. Delia was looking down at him in awe.

'We're both ex-policemen,' George explained. 'We've come across similar cases— it happens all the time. There's nothing to hang a hat on, but you *know*. There's a feeling to it. Dozens of tiny things coming together, but not evidence to parade in Court. It's how a lot of people get a not guilty verdict. Try persuading a jury. Just you try.'

'You've got it wrong, George,' I told him, gently chiding, aware that he was deliberately needling. 'Mr. Collis was found guilty. He was convicted, and sentenced to life imprisonment.'

'Then what . . .'

'The seven months!' Collis cried in triumph. 'Their barrister was too clever. One month and nineteen days between the first two deaths, two months and twenty-five days between the second and the third. And at the time of the trial I'd been in custody for seven months. And the prosecuting counsel tripped up. I reckon he knew he'd got a rotten case. He pointed out—and this was in his closing address—that

I'd been out of circulation for all of seven months, and there hadn't been any more. Now . . . wasn't that stupid of him! I got sentenced, but it was splendid grounds for appeal. On appeal, the conviction was quashed. That was a week ago. And here I am.'

'It would've been a good idea to be somewhere else,' George suggested.

'Oh no! No, no. Leave here? Be driven away? Not ever. This is my home. I designed and built it. They're not driving me out.'

'It could be unpleasant,' I said. 'Dangerous, even.'

'That's why I need you.'

'It can't have been pleasant for your wife, the past year.'

She looked at me in surprise. Collis glanced away. 'I have been terrified,' she admitted. 'For a while I went to my sister's, but I was afraid to leave the house empty. It all made me quite ill.' She spoke with quiet dignity.

'But it's over now,' Collis said with impatience.

Her voice was empty. 'Now that you're home, dear.'

'Over?' George demanded. 'How can it be over? Ever. Unless you go clear away and start a new life.'

'No,' Collis snapped.

'I was talking to your wife.'

'This is ridiculous. Did I ask you here to break up my marriage!'

13

'Don't be foolish, Adrian.'

'The man said . . .'

'He can see I don't intend to leave you.'

They looked at each other. She was calm, holding him, bolstering him. He was smiling when he turned to me, ignoring George.

'You can see I can't leave, and I desperately need your help.'

'You're safe here. You've got your dog— and the police are legally bound to give you protection.'

'Whatever they might feel about it,' said George softly.

'It's not here I'm worried about. These . . . people, the ones who pester us, they're not the real danger. It's Madge's father, Tina's step-father, and Marilyn's husband. I'll need you to guard me every minute of the day.'

'We'll keep an eye on you,' George promised.

'You mean, even away from here?' I asked Collis.

'Anywhere—any time. Do you think they've forgotten?'

'I shouldn't think they have.'

'What you want,' put in George heavily, 'and let's get this straight, is a full-time guard wherever you might be.'

'You're very quick.'

'I've been taking it all in.'

I could see that this would not do. If we were to work for this man, there had to be less tension between Collis and George. I'd sprung it on him, I admit, but I'd never known George so antagonistic. Collis looked at me, one eyebrow raised. Delia took George's glass from him and said something. There seemed no need for her to have bent so close. George grunted and levered himself to his feet. He plodded after her across to the drinks cupboard, and they seemed to be chatting about the painting.

I heard her say, '. . . our honeymoon in Paris. The showers . . .'

Collis spoke at my elbow. 'Can I see you alone for a minute.'

Then I understood what George was doing. His attitude had split us, but it had also split the husband and wife. We would have separate impressions to compare later. People tend to underestimate George.

I put down my empty glass on the top of a low and wide bookcase, and followed Collis. He led me through a side door into a small square room, which was obviously a workroom because it was dominated by one of those large easel-type drawing boards, with an automatic contraption on it for maintaining right angles for him.

There were drawings and plans everywhere, stacked on chairs, leaning in rolls against the walls, even, the smaller ones, in frames on the walls themselves. Also framed was the Certificate that Adrian Palmer Collis was an

Associate of the R.I.B.A.

I wondered how long he would be allowed to keep it.

He was standing at the uncurtained window, looking out at no more than his own reflection. I thought it was perhaps a bit risky, if what he'd said was true, but the boundaries were really too far away for the odd hurled brick.

He turned. The movement was an abrupt challenge.

'I'm not happy about your partner.'

'To tell you the truth, I'm not happy to be talking to you without having George here to listen. He's what you wanted. A guard. George is tough, and faster than he seems with all that bulk on him. Admitted he's not all that young, but he lasts the course . . .'

'You understand what I mean. There's more to it than just guarding, and I'm sure you know that.'

'Do I?' The framed drawing I was studying was of a bungalow set amongst trees, and seemingly constructed of logs. 'I like this, you know.' I turned. 'You have a fine style.'

'That's my design for a Forestry Commission hut, intended to house one Ranger and his family.'

'Intended?'

'It's not been completed. You're avoiding the issue.'

'I didn't like what I was thinking.'

'Tell me what you thought.'

16

His eyes were bright. There was an intensity of purpose about him that I found disquieting.

'I think we'd better not waste time with guessing games,' I said. 'Suppose you tell me, before George joins us.'

For a moment he held my eyes, before he looked away with a small laugh, very like contempt.

'You've just been admiring a symbol of it. That design for a log house—I assure you, perfectly practical—is just one building I shall never complete. If they ever find the funds to go on with it, do you think they'll come back to me? Do you really?' He gave a bark of disgust. 'Oh, there're still a few projects I'm working on—they can hardly break my contracts. But you can imagine the future. Leave here, you say. Start afresh. But where? And under what name? There'll be very few people like your friend, who will not know the name of Adrian Collis.'

'Then change it.'

'I can imagine that. I suppose I send my Certificate back to the R.I.B.A., and ask them to change my name? That'd be interesting— when I'm waiting to hear that they're thinking of striking me from their rolls.'

'Surely . . . now that the conviction's quashed . . . they couldn't . . .'

'I have brought disrepute. *I* have! My God, and I've done nothing. It's been done to me. Do you think that's fair, Mallin? Tell me you

17

think I have been treated fairly.'

The appalling thing about it was that he was speaking quietly, and in a level voice. It was as though he knew he had no need for dramatic emphasis; all his distress and disillusion were condensed into the bitterness of the words themselves.

'There's no reason to expect fairness from life.'

'A philosophy of despair, my friend. I've had nine months in which to study all the philosophies, and despair was the one I was fighting to reject. No—we don't give in, do we. We go on trying to recover something from the disaster. And do you know what I'm going to recover, Mr. Mallin? My innocence, that's what. You, with your big and somewhat unpleasant friend, are going to prove my innocence.'

'Now come on . . . after this time . . .'

'You're being obtuse. Deliberately, I'd say. The nine months is the operative thing. The prosecution used that period against me—only it was seven at the time. Now we will use it *for* me. As they said, there was no murder during that time. And why? Not, I assure you, because the murderer was in prison, but because the real murderer *knew* I was in prison. He was lying low, knowing that one more similar crime would not only help me, but would start the police looking around again. You get my point?'

I tried to hide my uneasiness. It would have been a terrible strain, the whole thing taken as far as a life sentence. It could have pushed him too far.

'No,' he said gently, 'I am not insane. I've simply had a long time to think it out. What— I'm asking you—do you think will happen now?'

I liked the way the trees in his log house sketch were done in little squared-off lines.

'Now,' I said, sighing, 'our sex murderer, who has somehow managed to restrain his repulsive urges all this while, will see his way clear. He'll have you around to lap up the blame, and he'll say to himself: oh, good-oh, I can have another go. Let's look around for some choice bit of . . .'

'I didn't ask you to be flippant.'

'You asked me to do some guessing, and I don't like the result,' I said angrily. 'It comes out that some innocent girl, somewhere around here, might well become a target, because *you're* here—'

'Now wait a minute . . .'

'Just you listen. It *will* be because you're still in the district, one way or another. If you leave, then maybe—just maybe—this sex-nut of ours, always assuming it's not you, may well continue to restrain himself. But no. You have to flaunt yourself. You, mister almighty, who's too proud to turn and run—you have to shove your neck out and pretend you're not

19

frightened. Of course you're not. It isn't you who stands to be raped and murdered.'

'A speech. I get a speech. You react. I thought you might be as gormless as the other.'

'What you need's a genius. Not me. Not George. A genius, who can work out who's going to be the next victim, and be there in time to prevent it.'

'Prevent it? Oh no, nobody can do that. Mark my words, there's going to be another. The weather is right, the mood is right. And when it happens—where will you be, you or your partner? You will be watching me, Mallin. Watching me, with positive evidence that I cannot have been the murderer this time, and therefore wasn't before.'

I didn't know whether he disgusted me or not. I just did not know. He could have been as shining-white innocent as he claimed, and be convinced, in all sincerity, that this was his only chance. Or it could be a trick. But all I could think was that, with all that suppressed and compressed emotion, not a bead of sweat had broken out on his face. Yet runnels were pouring down my back, creeping into my eyes, and blurring my vision.

I realised why he had said he anticipated it would be over soon. He expected another murder, or he intended one. And coolly waited.

He said: 'You appreciate the logic in this?'

'I appreciate it.'

'And you'll go along with me?'

'I'll do that. But not for your logic. Not even for you, Mr. Collis. But for that one slim chance that we might be around, when the next girl falls for a smile that could be as false as hell.'

He was very quick. 'You think that because I haven't ranted and raved, then I've been false with you?'

'No. I don't question your sincerity. It's too quiet to be denied.'

He raised his chin and his eyes were laughing. 'I think we might work well together, Mr. Mallin.'

It was then that we heard the woman's voice raised in a scream. It was joined by the unbroken blare of a car horn and the frantic baying of Major.

Together, we began to run.

CHAPTER TWO

George had a flying start, and justified my claim that he was more nimble than he seemed. On the way through I caught a brief glimpse of Delia, standing with her knuckles pressed against her mouth, her eyes staring.

The noise was coming from the gate, which Collis had padlocked behind us when we

21

arrived. Major was standing our side of it, supplementing the frantic efforts of a woman standing dimly beside a car just outside.

'For God's sake, Amanda,' Collis shouted, 'what's the matter?'

She seemed alone. Major desisted when we approached, and the woman took her hand from the horn. She came forward, wild, her hair flying.

'You damned fool, Adrian. What's the gate doing, fastened like this? Why'd you have to have a dog to add to it?' She was almost whimpering. She glanced round. 'They wouldn't go away. Oh dear God, open the gate.' She whirled and placed her back against the upper rail, raising her voice. 'Go away! Why don't you go away!'

I could see nothing in the heavy shadows beneath the trees. Collis was fumbling with his padlock. She fell through, almost into his arms. He muttered to her. I barely heard what he said. '. . . an exhibition of yourself . . . pull yourself together, my dear.'

I clearly heard her choked reply. 'You've got a lot to answer for.'

I said: 'Leave the key. We'll get the car in.' I wanted George to myself; I wanted the quiet country road to ourselves.

George stood at my elbow. He spoke quietly. 'Dave, what the hell've you got us into?'

'Let's take a good look.'

'I don't want to take a look at anything.'

But he walked out with me into the road. I reached inside and put off the car's lights, the better for our vision to adapt. We stopped, three feet apart, our eyes hunting. I was feeling that we were the hunted.

It was just possible to see that the nearest trees were winter-stripped silver birches, grey ghosts of the summer, behind them the rising and tightly-pressed trunks of the firs. Against the sky, barely lighter, the tufted heads stood silent and morose. Frost creaked. There were the usual rustles that run through stilled woodland, and a gentle, silent drift of frost dust from the branches.

When you stare at shadows, they move. Darkness slid from one tree to another. The frost drew deep, misty breaths. The white-rimmed blades of grass on the far side of the ditch made beckoning gestures as they slowly straightened.

Suddenly George raised his voice. 'Why don't you come out where we can see you! You scared or somethin'?'

His voice shook the frost and the echoes died in the distance. Then there was nothing but the silence again.

'Let's get the car in,' I said. George was furious. One hint and he'd dash off ridiculously into the trees.

He turned, his shoulders high. 'For Christ's sake, Dave!'

'Let it lie, George. I'll drive the car in. You padlock the gate.'

It was then I realised that Major was still sitting quietly in the open gateway. He did, indeed, appreciate the boundaries of his preserve. But his ears were high and his nostrils wide, every sense straining. When I came close I could hear the deep throb of a plaintive grumbling way down in his throat.

'Good boy,' I said, and he relaxed reluctantly.

A branch clattered along the roof of the car and rebounded from the gate. Major skipped aside and stared at it. Then he picked it up and ran off to show it to Collis.

'You padlock the gate, George,' I said firmly, and he growled.

Collis had left the front door open. When I got out of the car, George was guarding it with his back, blocking most of the light.

'Wait a minute,' he said.

'Later, George. There'll be time later.'

'What're we doing, protecting this bastard?'

'We don't know he's guilty.'

'Of course we know. He was *found* guilty.'

'All the same, are you going to walk away and leave him to it?'

'Did he seem scared to you? Damn it all, he's making a meal of it. You know the type, Dave. It makes 'em somebody. Important. D'you think he cares a jot for that little woman in there?'

Little woman! 'You managed to get your talk with her. So . . . what d'you think?'

'She's the one with the guts. She's the one trying to bear up. All *she* wants is to get as far away from here as she can.'

'But she's not about to do any such thing, and you know it. She's stubborn. A matter of principle. People with principles cause most of the trouble in this world. The woman's a damned nuisance.'

He bristled. 'I don't see why you should say that.'

'Because if it wasn't for her, you'd be able to walk away with a clear conscience. Now look at you, you big fool, all flabby with protective feelings. Oh come on, let's get inside.'

We trailed back to the big room. They were in there, the atmosphere tingling with tension, Major standing with his thawing branch ignored.

'Better get back on the job,' I told him, and we took his stick out of the front again.

When I returned, George had insinuated himself into the setting without disturbing the situation. Delia had mentioned a sister. This had to be the one; you could see the likeness, though Amanda, as Collis had called her, was clearly the elder, the more mature, but the more emotional. She was in the middle of a tirade.

'If I'd thought for one minute that you'd come back here . . . Whatever were you thinking about, Adrian? I could . . . for two pins I could hit you, if it'd knock some sense into your head.'

He shrugged, pursing his lips in amused deprecation. But his eyes were angry. He was seated on the arm of one of his easy chairs, a leg swinging free. Delia was smoking nervously, not looking at her sister. Amanda was the dominant one; Delia had to fall back on stubborn silence.

'Well!' said Amanda, looking from one to the other. 'Say something. Tell me at least what you intend to do.'

Collis spoke lightly, surprise in his voice. 'Pick up where I left off, of course. There are several projects . . . my office . . .'

'You talk as though things are normal!' she cried.

'Would it help if I went into hysterics?'

'You! What about Delia? Don't you ever give her one thought? Why don't you do what any decent man would do—take her away from here?'

For a moment I thought he would strike her. His leg was still. Then he slid from the arm of the chair and he could not hide the fury in his expression. She stood, daring him. But his self-mastery was superb; his voice was steady.

'You know why I can't leave.'

'Perhaps I do, Adrian. But you want to ask yourself why you can't leave. You need to get

26

that very straight.'

'Mandy!' said Delia sharply. For a second Amanda stood still, looking mockingly into Adrian's eyes, then slowly she turned to her sister. 'Mandy, please! This isn't your affair,' Delia pleaded.

'I'm not going to stand aside and watch you suffer.'

'Then do please go where you can't see me. I appreciate . . .' She paused, controlling her voice. 'I know you mean well. But Adrian will not leave . . .'

'The fool!'

'He will *not*. For a number of very good reasons.'

'Has he explained them?'

'You never married, Mandy, or you wouldn't have to ask. Adrian doesn't need to explain. I'm his wife. You might as well leave.'

'With things like this! With that . . . those creatures out there!'

'Please . . .' Delia whispered. 'Please go.'

Amanda tossed her head. Her hair was darker than Delia's, and she wore it longer. She was slimmer and more active, with the nervous activity of the emotional person, and her face was thinner. But her beauty was more finely-drawn, and the facial planes were balanced. Her eyes were beautiful.

With the toss of her head she threw away the mood. Perhaps she could see the distress she was inflicting on her sister. She was abruptly skittish.

'Silly me—rushing over here. I'm just too impetuous. I'll leave you lovely people. Who're your two heavy friends? No, don't tell me. Policemen. Oh dear, haven't I been indiscreet! How can you ever forgive me. Adrian, you're a dear.' She patted his cheek. 'Such a romantic creature. How can you stand him, Delia? I'll let myself out.'

Then she paused, aghast, and seemed chastened. She looked around.

'If you two gentlemen will see me to my car.'

We saw her into the road and away. She backed the old Morris Minor down the drive with verve and imprecision, and nearly took away the gatepost. We stood, coughing gently in the exhaust smoke, and watched the one tail-light disappear.

The trees absorbed the smoke. The night settled.

'Bossy,' decided George. 'I bet their mother died when they were very young.'

'Psychology, George?'

'*She* hasn't got any doubts. She's dead certain he did it.'

'Them. Three murders.' I glanced at him. 'And the little woman, George? What does the wife think? Did she say?'

'No. I don't think she cares. But I'm sure she knows. I hope you're not expecting any enthusiasm from me, Dave.'

'You don't have to be keen. Just do your

protecting bit.' I decided it wasn't a good time to tell him about the other bit. 'You know you'll do it.'

'I might be just that bit slower. Not being too keen.'

He stamped back into the bungalow.

Collis had it all worked out. I couldn't help thinking of George's claim that Collis was enjoying it. Every detail had been slotted-in with superfluous care. When we were to pick him up, how we were to follow him discreetly, where we were to park at his office block, even, by heaven, how we'd arrange our shifts.

'Suppose you leave it to us,' I said. George was sitting forward dangerously on the edge of one of the not-so-easy chairs, his face inscrutable, his eyes on Delia.

'As long as it's done,' Collis conceded.

'You'll never be out of our sight—one or the other of us.'

'I did say discreetly.'

'Shadows,' I assured him. 'As inobtrusive as shadows.'

'Yes, I see.' He cleared his throat. 'If I anticipate long journeys, I'll try to slip you messages.'

'In code?' George murmured, reacting.

'It shouldn't be too obvious we're connected,' Collis reproved him.

George raised his eyes, but fortunately kept his comments to himself, at least until we were alone. We'd been alone for ten minutes,

29

driving back to town, before he even spoke. Getting well clear, I suppose.

'You can see why they charged him.'

Collis wasn't quite real, not as a protagonist in this situation. Somewhere along the line he'd rationalised it. Now it had the romantic savour of a lone struggle against adversity, with two doubtful assistants, and an eventual triumph. He couldn't wait for it.

The fact that what he saw as his triumph could arise only from another girl's death preyed heavily on my mind. My conscience, even. I was a party to it.

George's comment was a mile back down the road when I admitted: 'I can see. But perhaps he wasn't so bad, then.'

'He's hovering on the edge of insanity, Dave. He wants putting away. Obviously he did in those three girls.'

'I don't know. If so, why'd he expect us to prove he didn't?'

He was silent for a moment. 'Does he? There's something you haven't told me.'

I explained what it was. I could feel him staring at me in disbelief.

'And you agreed to help him with that?'

'What else could I do? He's probably right—there'll be another.'

'That's real dandy. And we sit around, waiting for it to happen?'

'That's the general idea.'

'You must be going soft. He's conned you.

Of *course* there'll be another, because he'll do it himself.'

'Not if we watch him closely enough.'

'He's got it all planned! This time he'll have an alibi, something crafty, and we're the mugs who're going to give it to him.'

'If we let it happen like that.'

'You're so damned complacent, Dave. What's got into you?'

'Just a little bit of disgust, rumbling away in my guts. I don't like the feeling, and it's not going away until I *know*. So we wait and we watch, and we do a few quiet enquiries, and if we come up with proof that he's conning us, then, George, he'll wish he'd gone down for that life sentence.'

'Enquiries!' George was vehement. 'Not me mate. I'm going to be watching that smarmy hypocrite. Do your own damned enquiring.'

George is not subject to persuasion when he gets an idea in his head. To tell the truth, I wasn't prepared to argue with him. I had been playing it down. I'd read the trial transcript, you see, and the plain truth was that Collis had not mentioned a tenth part of the evidence against him. All circumstantial, I admit, but as sound as a signed confession.

George said: 'You're not thinking of staying in town?'

'Where the action is. Where else?'

And where, also, at that small centre, but at the Crown? It was the only place that could call itself an hotel.

We had come in to the square down a long hill flanked by large and obscured residences. They grew their greenery sufficiently tall to blunt the impact of the surroundings. The main square was barely large enough to accommodate an island where the five main roads met. The traffic was chaotic, with five sets of traffic lights and no apparent co-ordination. The shopping centre was dull and dingy. The Crown, the other side of the square, didn't look any more encouraging.

George remarked that they'd never find a room for us there. But they did, a double room over the public bar, so that there was no possibility of rest until after closing time.

This fact was likely to be awkward for us. There would have to be shifts, one of us always sleeping at strange hours.

'I've been in worse,' said George, but when he sat down heavily on the bed I thought it was going through the floor.

'Let's see if we can get a sandwich and a drink,' I suggested. 'And then we toss to see who gets to Firbelow at six in the morning.'

But there was going to be no doubt about that. I was the one with the car.

'It's your car,' he said, grinning.

'Don't imagine you're getting out of all the work. We'll get you a car.'

'We'll never hire one around here.'

'Buy one, George. You'll need a car, and

we've got Elsa's money.'

'We can't . . .'

But we could. Elsa, my wife, who's got all the money, had decided to diversify her investments, and had put some capital into our agency. It was not very complimentary, really, that she had done it as soon as George joined me in the firm. But it was all legal, with a contract and interest clauses, and heaven help us if we were a day late with the repayments.

Logically, it was a sound investment to buy George a car. But he seemed to think I was offering him some sort of a bribe.

'It's *our* money, not mine,' I said, annoyed.

We were still arguing when we entered the public bar, which, I suppose, was the reason we failed to notice the impression we made. George was lifting a pint of bitter when he detected the silence. We looked round casually.

At this early hour there were only about twenty in there, all men, the lonely perhaps or the unhappy, reluctant to part from workmates and get off home. They were eyeing us quietly, their glasses stilled. A bad sign, that.

There was a rustle. 'That's them!' Something like a sustained growl. They moved, fanning out and advancing.

'You tell 'em, Jonas,' one of them said, the encourager, the one who remains at the rear, craning and grinning.

They pushed Jonas forward. He was a big

33

man, could even have been a miner in his youth; he would be in his forties, I thought. Now . . . well, a bricklayer, perhaps. He had roughened, red hands and the wind-bruised face of a man who works outdoors. He was wearing blue jeans and a black turtleneck sweater, with a donkey jacket over it. His chest was big, though with a barrel that does not denote strength but more likely weak lungs. Emphysema. Possibly a pit legacy. He moved ponderously, his mouth moving, pausing only to spit sideways.

'Who's this?' said George quietly.

Jonas? 'It'll be Jonas Fletcher,' I said. 'The girl Tina's father. Or step-father, I think. She was seventeen, George.'

'A strange, startled girl,' he whispered.

'What you up to?' Fletcher demanded, spreading his legs. 'We don't want you around here.'

They applauded with groans, half-empty glasses being lifted in agreement, full ones being moved gently.

I told him we were pleased to meet him. 'I was going to look you up, anyway. Some questions . . .'

'You can keep away from me. I'm warnin' you. I got me a gun.'

'You give 'em a barrel-full,' the encourager shouted.

'What'll I do, Dave?' George asked softly. 'Swat him?'

But they'd heard. The one at the back had ears like garage doors. 'What about that, Jonas. Think he can swat you?'

'You buy him a drink, George,' I said. 'I've got business to attend to.'

If you walk right at them when they've only got their solidarity to cling to, they part. They hesitate, and then it's too late, because you're in amongst them, and then through. They parted as though I was launching a ship. I reached the encourager and lifted the glass from his fingers, placing it carefully on a table.

'I don't think we need you, friend. How about taking a little walk outside?'

He gulped, and poked at my chest. I think he only intended to emphasise something, but an extended finger is inviting. I seized it and twisted it, and his arm came round, then I took it to the outer door and tossed it into the street. He went with it.

'Now,' I said. 'Where were we?'

There was complete silence. The barman was drawing a pint, and he slid it towards Jonas Fletcher. He took it up with care, and deliberately poured it onto the floor. Then, his point made, he turned and marched out, searching perhaps for encouragement.

'Rumble, rumble,' they all said, nodding to each other, their honour satisfied.

George shook his head. 'It's only postponing it, you know. He's the sort that has to be thumped some time or other.'

35

'But I wanted to ask him something. Quietly.'

'Ask him what?'

'Why his step-daughter, who sounds as though she was a nervous little thing, should be out on a dark February night on a dark February road. The police failed to raise even a hint of a boy-friend.'

'Girls do funny things. They don't have to have reasons.'

'True,' I agreed.

But there had been a small gain. I at least knew the name of our encourager. It had been spoken, sarcastically, by his nearest neighbour when I grasped his finger. 'You show him, Reuben.'

He was Reuben Goldwater, the father of Madge, who had died on the 4th January. I should have kept hold of that finger. There were questions, too, for Goldwater, when I could get round to it.

CHAPTER THREE

It was quite a while before I did. Six days later I was sitting in the Porsche watching the office, and talking to George. George, at that time, should have been driving over to relieve me— but nevertheless I was talking to him. The money wouldn't go as far as inter-car radios, once we'd acquired the Renault 20TL, so we had compromised on a tape recorder. It gave us something to talk and listen to during the long waiting hours, even if there was still, drearily, nothing to report.

A parked car can become very cold in winter. The frost continued; the mists returned every evening. I wondered whether Collis was waiting for a specially thick one before trying to slip our leash. But there was no sign of impatience from him. In fact, he was treating the whole thing as a glorious adventure.

I was backed into a parking space marked G. Plummer, to one side of the L-shaped parking area. G. Plummer, I understood, was fortunately visiting Brazil at that time. Directly opposite me was the yellow BMW 2500 that Collis used. Two floors up, and within my vision, was the window of Collis's office, which he occupied alone. From time to time he would appear at the window and wave idiotically. A little to one side was the main entrance, and I could even see down the side of the building, where the side door opened onto a narrow alleyway. There were only the two office entrances—we had checked it. Two entrances to the actual car park, too, opening into adjacent streets, but no way out of the actual building without being spotted.

It was the ideal spot, and the only one which afforded such an advantage, most of the car park being round the corner.

On the seat beside me was the tape recorder. In the glove compartment was the fourth of Collis's coy little secret messages, a sketch of Coventry Cathedral. I had been listening to George's comments.

'. . . *another damned picture, and he had the cheek to tuck it into my top pocket. Is he crazy or something? I'd gone into the bungalow—you know how he invites you in, all secret glances up and down the road—went in and had a cup of tea with the missus, and he could've told me. Just said: Coventry today. But no. Not our Collis. I tell you, Dave . . .*'

I recorded for him:

'*Don't let it upset you, George.*'

Snapped it off and thought, and added:

'*Just watch him that much closer.*'

I didn't think Collis was stupid. Whatever he had in mind would be subtle and carefully planned.

Apart from the diversions of his messages, everything had been quiet. Still the watchers came at night, though we saw no positive evidence to bolster the eerie awareness. Still we were treated to animosity wherever we went. Everybody knew why we were there.

All I could pray was that George would not relax. But George is a man of action, and waiting would be a strain. I had noticed that Delia was no longer the 'little woman'. Perhaps she was not pleading for his help.

He came at 4.30. It was George's turn to

follow Collis the twenty-five motorway miles back home, and stay there until I joined him at nine. We would patrol until the feeling of observation disappeared.

George hoisted the green Renault up the slope from East Street, and I eased out of the space to allow him to back in. I leaned against his lowered window.

'What's she done at you, George? It's his missus all of a sudden.'

'I asked her—you know, kind of slipping it in . . .' I nodded; he can be as subtle as an avalanche when he tries. 'I asked her if she believed he'd killed those girls.'

'And?'

'She just stared at me as though I was mad and said: "That isn't the point." What sort of crazy answer is that?'

'A woman's answer, George.'

'They're both crazy.'

I laughed and left him to it. There was just time, before they left, to get to the Council Offices.

This was one of the reorganised offices which had resulted from the shuffling of boundaries. It had caused young Andy Partridge to buy a motorcycle in order to get to work, when previously he had had only a ten minute walk to his local office. Andy Partridge was the widower of Marilyn Partridge, the third young woman to die, and it had seemed a good idea to intercept him as he left work.

39

Up to that point he was an enigma to me. All my information was of his quiet disposition, his calmness, and his patience. If he had wept over his wife's murder, he had done it alone.

The car park of the old red brick council office was down a side street. There were six motorcycles in the park, either of two Honda 200s being possibly his. But when they all streamed out, the owners of both bikes were nothing like the description I had. It seemed I had wasted my time.

But not quite. My passenger's door opened and a slim, lithe shape slid in beside me. I turned to him politely.

'I take it there's a reason for this.'

'Partridge is sick,' he told me. 'Been on the box for more than a week now.'

'You don't say.'

'Detective Sergeant Williamson,' he introduced himself. 'Just thought I'd save you some trouble.'

'It's very good of you.'

'Not at all.' He was polite, but not looking at me. 'You can take it easy, Mallin. We've got it in hand.'

'Got what in hand?'

'The Collis business.'

'Police protection?'

'Something like that.'

'Only like it. You can't touch him again, and you know it. Not even if he gave a full

40

admission to the Sunday papers.'

'The Super was annoyed, losing him like that.'

'But there's nothing you can do to him.'

'Perhaps not. Not for the first three, anyway.'

And with a nod and the nearest he could get to a smile, he slid out and walked back to his own car. As I watched him in the rear-view mirror, an old Morris Minor crossed behind, and turned away.

Her surname was Greaves, I had discovered. Amanda Greaves. I had not seen her since that first meeting, but something Collis had said indicated that she had been to see her sister twice. But he had not told me she worked for the council.

I was doing some fast to and fros to get round after her. It could be useful to know where she lived. As I got the car turned, Williamson stood out in the street and waved me down.

I wound down the window, the better to curse him.

'Riverside Court,' he said. 'Flat 27. She's secretary to the County Planning Officer. Save you the trouble.'

I took him at his word—I had lost her, anyway—and went to see whether Andy Partridge was sick enough to be home.

Six days, and I haven't found time to chat to anybody. What with the organisation and all

41

the detail work, and buying the Renault for George, there had hardly been a spare minute. The trouble with George is that he's so big. I am five feet eleven, and no scraggy object, but he makes me look puny. So it had to be a sizeable car, and though I hadn't said so, we were left with two fast cars—my Porsche and Collis's BMW—and George's Renault, which was still being run in. As I saw it, if Collis was intending to give one of us the slip, one misty night along the motorway, it was going to be George. So it had been six days of worry for me, and with none of the background filled in.

Andy Partridge was cleaning his motorbike in the yard, a 200 Honda, as I'd been told, which is a nice, cobby bike. His thin face was peeked with the cold, his eyes watering.

'I'm Mallin,' I said.

'I know.' He considered me, slowly straightening. 'You people will do anything for money.'

'Within reason. I heard you were sick.'

'I get this catarrh.' He gestured with his oily rag towards the Honda. 'I need fresh air. All I can get.'

In that case, you'd think he would get a job on a farm. There were plenty of farms around there; the house he lived in was a farm cottage, which he was renting. He now lived alone, a half mile from his nearest neighbour, who would be Jonas Fletcher, along a minor road that carried hardly any traffic.

'I suppose they say that Collis could've taken a short cut along here,' I said conversationally. 'From the motorway.'

'The best way to Collis's place—it's four miles from here—would be from junction 7. But I suppose he *could* have used junction 6, and cut through Allesley and Lower Boreton.'

'But you're not convinced?'

'If I had been, I'd have killed him. Wouldn't I?'

'Would you?'

I considered him doubtfully. He was in his early twenties, not more than five feet seven and lightly-built with it. He had a long face, his mouth all teeth, his eyes that roe deer brown, soft and inoffensive. He appeared nervous, his hands moving all the while. I had not yet seen him at the Crown, amongst our tormentors.

'Would you?' I repeated, and he shook his head, baffled, doubting his ability. What worried me was that he could not have doubted it unless he had considered it, and such a person, giving calm thought to such a possible action, is infinitely more dangerous than a wild and unmotivated ruffian. He saw I had realised this, and gave a twisted grimace before he went on:

'When she died—when they came and told me—I was wild then. I could have done anything to the swine who'd done *that* to her, if he'd been in front of me, and I'd got my hands on him. The thing was outside control. That

43

was then, for an hour, for a day, perhaps a week. After that—you know—it goes. The fury and the . . . the distress.' He threw the rag away from him. 'They're saying I'm a coward, because I didn't go to him, to Collis, like Fletcher did, and even Goldwater, and shout filthy words and threats in his face. He was in custody then. It's easy with a copper holding each arm, and if you're so sure you're right.'

'But you're not sure?'

'Not sure enough to blow his head off with a shotgun, say.'

'He could've come past here. It was late . . . ten-ish . . . and the time fitted. He didn't get home before one . . .'

'Where was he in between?'

'Driving, perhaps, recovering until he was fit enough to be seen by his wife. Wives are apt to see things.'

'I know. My wife did. Things that weren't there.'

'Ah!'

'What the hell's that mean? Ah! What wonderful thing've I admitted? That my wife thought I was having an affair—so what? She wanted us to leave here—this cottage. But I like it here. There's plenty of air. Not much of anything else . . . no mains water for instance, and no phone . . . but she wanted to go and live with her mother. Apron strings complex, and she'd row about anything to try and push the issue on. Then, when they moved the offices, that was a thing she could throw at me, my extra journey. And her mother lives only about a mile from the new offices.'

'Why're you telling me this?'

'Because you're working round to asking what she was doing out on a quiet side road like this, with only a mac over her pyjamas and dressing-gown.'

'I wasn't. But it's something that's never been fully explained.'

'She was going to the phone box on the Lower Boreton road, to call her mother. We'd had another row, all evening, and I went to bed early for some peace. But no, she'd got to come after me, and so's not to encourage her, I pretended to be asleep, and off she went to phone mommy.'

'And you didn't go after her?'

'Hell no! Any row we had, and it was always dash off and phone mommy. Anyway, I'd pretended so hard, that I really was asleep. It was the copper at the door who woke me up.'

'And Collis, taking his short cut from junction 6, came across her, all alone, in her nightwear? It sounds very feasible.'

'It's too late to collect evidence against him now.'

'I was looking for something in his favour.'

'You won't get it from me.'

'But I have, you know. Perhaps you patched up the quarrel before you went off to sleep.'

'I don't get your point.'

'Think about it.'

I left him to his thinking. He got it as I shut the gate behind me.

'You lousy bastard!' he shouted, and he threw a spanner at me.

That was all I had time for that day. Back to the Crown, a change and a quick meal, a quiet hour, then it was out to join George at Firbelow. The night was bitter and there was cloud massing on the far horizon. Snow, I thought, just what we need!

Now there was only the taint of hatred in the trees. The cold was winning the battle for Collis.

It was my turn to pick him up the next morning. At seven I was there, invited in, as usual, for ten minutes in his workroom, and then away. He could have told me where it was to be that day, but we had to have the old cloak and dagger game. This time it was a simple sketch of a fir tree. Intriguing.

'Why the devil can't you say . . .'

He grinned at me. In the past few days he had grown more confident, quiet with it, his eyes steady. Delia was a passive shadow in the background. Major barely moved from her side during daylight. There had been a few minutes with her while he changed his tie, or something.

'I hope you're not going to let him down,' she said quietly.

'We don't intend to.'

46

'Since you came, he's been . . . well, changed. As though he knows there's an end in sight.'

I kept the chill from my voice. 'It's very flattering.'

'He's withdrawing even more, though. Never notices anything. He hasn't asked where Smoke has gone.'

'I beg your pardon.'

She lifted her hand in apology. 'You wouldn't know, of course. We had a grey, short-haired tom that we called Smoke. The day Major came, he disappeared. I think the dog's eaten him.'

I grimaced. There had been a flat, accepting tone to her voice. She had been battered beyond feeling. 'I doubt that. He'll have gone into hiding.'

'I was devoted to Smoke.'

'But now you have Major.'

She pulled his ear. 'It's not the same. I've got Adrian back, but *he*'s not the same.' And she turned away as Collis appeared.

I followed him, as before, to his office, and sat an hour in Plummer's parking space, and then we set out to solve the fir clue. It was simply a visit to the half-finished log house he had been building for the Forestry Commission. In effect, we were re-tracing our journey, though this site, although within the boundaries of the Chase, was a good ten miles from Firbelow, way up on the slopes of the opposite side of the valley.

I got out to follow him around. He permitted that, as the place was so deserted. It was up one of the Rides, which would have been impossible if the ground had not been hard with frost. He was lyrical over the design, and wistful over the possibility of re-commencing work on it. But the financial climate was not too encouraging. I couldn't see why we had come.

Half was fully constructed—a normal brick structure with half-log cladding to give the effect.

'You could've come up here,' I said.

'What?' He stopped, turned, and stared at me.

'In each case, all three murders, you got home very late, two or three hours after the estimated time of death.'

'Are you interrogating me?'

'Trying to clear my conscience.'

He gave a twisted smile. 'I'm employing you to clear mine.'

'You know about your own.'

He was disappointed in me. 'I was playing with words.'

'You're playing with me, avoiding it. I said: you could've come up here. To recover. To clean yourself up.'

'There was no blood,' he said in an even voice. 'In none of the murders was there any sign of that sort of violence.'

48

'Only strangulation—and sex. You're arguing against yourself. All right, so you wouldn't need to clean up. But what does it do to a man, that sort of thing? Or don't you know? But there'd be a need of time to become normal again. Normal enough to face a wife.'

'And you think I brought you here for that, to show you where I might have come to recover?'

'Your attitude has been strange.'

'Perhaps I was testing your loyalty.'

There was a bit of a snap in my voice. 'You might expect blind loyalty from your wife, Mr. Collis. But you won't get it from us. Not for money. We need something better than that.'

'And there was I, convinced I'd persuaded you.'

'Intrigued, not persuaded.'

'I thought you chaps did anything for money.'

It was the same attitude as Andy's. 'We spend a lot of time trapping the people who do.'

'Always with success, I hope.'

'Not always, even though greed's a simple motive to detect. Sex is rather more difficult. It's so very private.'

I saw I had destroyed some of his confidence in me. I was supposed to do things, but not ask why.

'We'll go back the other way,' he said,

dismissing me from his calculations. Then he threw up his head challengingly. 'The other way! It can lead us past Goldwater's place, past Fletcher's, even past Andy Partridge's. Now . . . doesn't that give you ideas, Mallin?'

I was walking away. I paused, hands deep in the pockets of my motoring coat. 'It makes me think you might just have been insane enough.'

He laughed, and we drove away.

I told George about it, late that night at the Crown. He just grunted. George was becoming impatient with it all.

'I told you not to do any digging,' he said.

Which, it turned out, was a little hypocritical of him.

I had seen Jonas Fletcher quite a few times at the Crown, but I wanted him alone. I hadn't been far wrong about the bricklaying. He was employed at a brickworks, a relic of the old East No. 6 Colliery, where they'd made bricks originally from the pit waste. I cornered him behind one of the kilns.

'What's it to you?' he demanded. 'Why'd you have to get in the way?'

'We're being paid to get in the way. And if you mean that if we weren't, you're going to lynch him—you and your mates—then I just don't believe it.'

'What ya on about?'

'The intentions you might have in mind.'

He frowned. Inferences were not his strong point. He shook his head. 'Who's said about

50

lynchin'? That's plain daft.'

'But one night, when you've got enough beer in you, you're going to march up to that place of his and do something violent. Because that's what you are, Fletcher, a violent man.'

It inflamed him. 'Yeah . . . and so what! What'd you do, if she'd been your kid?'

'Tina wasn't your child. She was your step-daughter.'

'To me . . . after her mother died . . . there was only us two. Tina was five, then. My kid, I tell ya. It's how she was to me. I treated her as a daughter.'

'Brought her up right, I bet. Taught her how to behave. Gave her the strap when she deserved it. Good old-fashioned discipline.'

'She wunna goin' to bring nothin' into my house.'

'Such as disgrace, I suppose. Was that likely?'

He stood, baffled, unable to control the conversation. 'We're good people round here, mister.'

'Of course you are. No scandal. So . . . there was a boy-friend, was there?'

'She was only sixteen, damn you!' he shouted. 'What ya think?'

'I think there'd be a boy-friend. It's a classical situation. The bullying and unimaginative father; the frightened child with a growing awareness of her sexuality.' He was frowning, turning his bull-head sideways to

51

consider me. 'She'd have to have some relief.'

'I'd've killed her.'

'Then why was she out on a dark February night—a year ago almost exactly? Tell me that.'

'What're y' sayin?'

'That you might have been using some of your discipline. That she'd run out of the house, frightened, and simply walked . . . anywhere.'

And he said something I did not understand, in a tone almost of triumph. 'But she'd be back.'

'What's that got to do with it?'

He tapped the side of his nose knowingly.

'She didn't get the chance to come back,' I said, annoyed.

'Not my fault.'

'For God's sake, man!'

'It was *his* fault, that Collis bleeder. But I'll get him. You just tell that big bloody mate o' yours, I'll still get him, gun or no gun.'

'*Now* what do you mean?'

'Come round to my place, bold as you like, chucking his questions around. Thinks he's tough, that un. Tried to push me around. On about why'd she go out, like I was her keeper or summat. I told him to clear off. Stuck me shotgun under his nose.'

'Then what'd he do?'

He wagged his huge hands. 'Took me by surprise. Grabbed it off me. And laughed.'

George would. I could see him doing it. I asked George about it the first opportunity I got, and he was big enough to look embarrassed. He was struggling into the shroud he calls his pyjamas.

'No investigation!' I mocked him. 'Who said that?'

'Well . . . I got to thinking.'

'You always do, given time.'

'I'm not too old to push that grin off your face, Dave.'

'I'm not going to dispute that. And have you seen Goldwater, too?'

'Start a thing, you've got to finish it.'

'Nothing about all this on tape, George.'

'This was for me, mate. Just because it's me who's uneasy.'

'And me, George. Tell me about Madge Goldwater.'

He looked grave, this being a general lowering of the jowls.

'The first one, as you know. The most natural, really. She's the only one with any sort of reason for being out when she was. The father thinks there was a boy-friend, but he's the sort that doesn't know anything about his family, and couldn't care less. The mother . . .'

'There's a mother?' I really shouldn't have assumed otherwise.

'That's right, you haven't even heard of her. She's that sort . . . negative. Goldwater's a natural coward, but he could terrify his womenfolk to his heart's content. You seen where they live? No? He's a farmworker, living half-way up the farm drive in an ancient tied cottage. Quiet there. Madge could've walked down to the road to meet anybody. Probably did. Met somebody she perhaps knew but didn't expect. It suits Goldwater to assume it was Collis. Then he can point his nasty muck-stained finger at somebody, and go along with the herd. But he won't *do* anything, Dave. He's too scared.'

'Scared of what?'

He shrugged. I'd never seen him so depressed.

'I tell you, Dave, I want to get out of this business. Collis fits—fits every way you look at it. And what are *we* supposed to be doing? Protecting? From what? There was a bit of mob frightening, but that's dropped off. And three bereaved heroes! My God—look at 'em. Jonas Fletcher, there's a tough type for you, but he's got to have the right backing, and the right opportunity, and the right amount of beer in him.'

'And a weapon,' I said quietly.

He went on as though I had not spoken. 'And Reuben Goldwater, scared of his own shadow. No danger there. Andy Partridge? He's too thoughtful and too quiet, and too undecided.'

'He could make up his mind.'

'What're you splitting hairs for, Dave! You

know the conclusion we've got to come to.'

'You're saying that we're wasting our time as protectors.'

'Well then.'

'But what of the other, eh George?'

'It's what I mean!' he said violently. 'Another sex assault and murder. That's a nice thing to sit and wait for. It's making my guts ache. I feel old and useless and bloody feeble.' He changed his tone abruptly. 'Did you know we're being followed?'

'*We* are?'

'Or him.'

'I've seen nothing. The police . . .'

'No. I'd know, in that case. This is just a feeling. No specific car. It's weird. Perhaps I'm not up to this, Dave. I want to pack it in.'

This was bad. I didn't look at him. 'If we go, it would still happen. The only difference'd be that we wouldn't be involved. That wouldn't be much comfort.'

'It's the waiting.'

'I know.'

'If he does it again . . . and we're around, that'd be . . .'

'The end of the waiting, George. And this time we'd nail him good and proper.'

He stared at me. 'I envy you, Dave.' He punched his pillow into submission.

It was my turn to lie in. George got out of the room with his usual attempt at silence, leaving me dozing and worried, and I was even later than I'd arranged with the landlord for my breakfast. It was well after ten when the phone rang behind the bar.

'It's your mate.'

I was round there fast. It had not previously been necessary to phone in.

'George?'

'Dave, I need your help.'

He could have reached through and hit me in the face. It was his tone, the utter despair and self-condemnation.

'What is it?'

'I've lost him. So help me, it's happened.'

But this time it was different. It was early morning, with many hours to darkness. Time to find him again.

'Where are you?' I said, and, strangely for George, he was for a moment confused.

'The phone box says Filsby 73.'

'*Where* George? You must know.'

There was a pause. His voice was low. 'I'm lost. Somewhere on the Chase. Ring the Post Office, they'll tell you. But get out here fast, Dave.'

'I will.' I hung up. The landlord was staring at me. 'Is there somewhere called Filsby?'

His eyes switched to the glass he was polishing. 'You don't want to be going there. It's where they found little Tina.'

56

CHAPTER FOUR

I should have given it some thought, made a few phone calls perhaps, and consulted a map. But instinct takes over, and all I did was run for the Porsche and head out towards Filsby.

It was snowing, those first languorous flakes that melt into the wet tarmac. But where I was heading it would be colder, with the snow lying. There had been enough in George's voice to persuade my foot hard down on the throttle. We flew.

He was waiting outside the phone box, stamping his feet. The snow was beginning to nestle in the astrakhan collar of his huge, midnight tent of a coat. I had run into and out of Filsby in five seconds. It was no more than a dairy farm on a bend and a low bridge over a stream down below, and three houses crouching behind a derelict church. We were completely surrounded by firs, which hissed as the snow lighted on them.

George said: 'He's done it.'

I slammed the door. 'Done what? Given you the slip, is that what you mean? It's what we've been waiting for. What happened?'

'Plummer was back from Brazil, that's all. There was me . . .'

'From the beginning, George.'

He waved his arm, but then restrained

himself. 'From the beginning,' he agreed heavily. 'The bungalow. I went there. The usual thing. Five minutes in his workroom and then on the road.'

'No cute little messages?'

'No. Just the twenty-five miles down the motorway to his office. I pulled in after him, and a red MGB was in Plummer's parking place. Collis was in his own car, parked, and what could I do? I drove on, round the corner, looking for another slot. Get out, I thought, and go back, and stand by the MGB. But I didn't get time. You can see past the building from round there, and along East Street, and what I saw was the BMW easing off and away. We're wasting time, Dave.'

'What's another few minutes? Go on.'

'So I said to myself, you cunning devil, Collis. Only ten seconds with my eye off him, and he'd acted. His brain must have been tuned in . . . Anyway, I drove back through the car park, and sure enough his car'd gone, and I pushed it a bit, thinking he'd be breaking his neck to get clear. But oh no, not on your life. There he was, a steady thirty, and not trying, Dave. Can you understand that?'

'Perhaps he wasn't intending to drop you. He'd maybe remembered an appointment.'

'I figured that. It'd started to rain—the sleety stuff. He just tooled along, onto the motorway again, and back towards home.'

'You were recording this?'

'One hand on the wheel, yes. For the record. Anyway, past junction 6 we go, past 7, and I was beginning to think: the Airport. Gonna take a plane and rape somebody in Hamburg, or something.' He shrugged. 'I was plain baffled, and trying out any daft idea, and the visibility was getting worse. He was steadily speeding up. Sixty, then seventy. The Renault's new, Dave, and stiff. I was dead worried. Then there's these two long trailer jobs, tagging each other in the middle lane, with ten yards of spray each side, and he pulled out to overtake. Me, I eased back a bit. I wasn't intending to ram him, in that lot. But then I got past and out in the clear, and there was no damn sign of him.'

'He'd slipped inside.'

'Dave, I knew. There were junction signs coming up, so he'd pulled over into the slow lane. I had to do the same, but damn it, I was in front. You can see the point.'

I did. George had been manoeuvred. But it didn't have to be deliberate. 'You had no alternative but to pull off at the next junction.'

'And stop, and wait for him, and watch him blind past in the outside lane, leaving me standing. Innocent, Dave, he could claim that.'

'Perhaps it was.'

He shook his head stolidly. His fury was well contained. 'It was smooth. Fooled me. I got down on the motorway again, but he was way out of sight. I pushed it. Lord, that temperature gauge! But no sign of him when I got to the next junction, so I pulled off and started looking.'

'Hopeless.'

'No. I was dead lucky. A lad on a pushbike said he'd gone past, described the BMW, yellow car going like mad, he said, and heading south. Back here, Dave, back to the Chase where the others have been. I could've killed him.'

'We don't know . . .'

'Of course we bloody know. I know, because I couldn't just stand here, waiting. I phoned Plummer Associates, Dave. Plummer's still in Brazil, and there was no MGB in his space when they looked out for me. That Collis is real smart. He used that ten second opportunity, when I'd got my eyes off him.'

'But he didn't try to ditch you. It was too casual.'

'I know, I know. Don't you think I've been driving myself mad, trying to make sense of it. But however it is, he's on the loose, and *here*. This is the Chase, Dave.'

'They found Tina down by that little bridge.' I didn't think I'd said it aloud.

He took a deep breath. 'Let's go and get him.'

'It's daylight. He'd have to wait. Sit and wait. It doesn't sound like a sex thing to me. Do they wait . . . hours . . . sit in the cold all day?'

'How the hell would I know what they do?'

'And I've got an idea where he'd go, anyway.'

'How can you?'

'He showed me, George. He couldn't have had any other reason, because there's no chance of starting work on it again.'

'On what?'

'His log house. Let's have a look at a map.'

We spread it on George's bonnet, because it's flat. The engine was ticking as it cooled. Ordinary road maps are no use with areas like the Chase, and we had brought Ordnance Surveys. The roads were marked as sinuous snakes, and there were large areas with none. The Rides were dotted double lines, straighter and more direct, and apparently purposeless. I studied it.

'There,' I decided, prodding a pencil at the intersection of two Rides. 'Now, let's see where we are now.'

'But . . . what'd he gain? The whole point was to use us as his alibi. Otherwise it's all insane.'

'I don't know. I don't understand him. Can you see Filsby?'

We didn't get the chance. A white and duck-egg green patrol car eased in gently behind us, and Sgt. Williamson unfolded himself from inside.

'You take off like a rocket,' he complained. 'And leave my men standing. We've hogged the air for half an hour, tracing you up here.'

'Very flattering,' I said.

'So he's on the loose!' But he was smiling.

'He's somewhere.'

Now it was almost a laugh, with his teeth showing and his eyes dancing. 'He's got himself a right pair, I must say. You know where he is? I'll tell you. He's where he's supposed to be . . . back at his office.'

'There'd be no point . . .' George's voice was rising angrily. I caught his arm.

'Do you know that?' I demanded.

'He phoned the Station to report his car had been stolen. I was there at the time.'

George roared: 'I followed . . .'

'There's something fishy here,' I put in. 'He could have used a tape, on that phone. Timed it.'

Amused, pursing his lips, Williamson was slowly shaking his head. 'He answered questions. Said he'd got up to his office and saw it going off down East Street, with the big, dumb oaf tailing it.'

George moved. I trod on his foot.

'His words,' the sergeant assured him, but the smile had gone sour.

'But you're not going to use up half an hour of radio messages over a stolen car,' I said softly.

'Well now . . .' He pulled his ear lobe. 'We've got an image to keep clean. The neutral coppers. We don't want anybody

62

saying we're hounding him, because we've always got one man in the offing.'

'So you think you'll recover his car for him,' I suggested.

George cleared his throat. 'Just as though he's not a triple murderer, and you're all mad that he slipped the net.'

Williamson's eyes bulged at him. 'Something like that. And seeing you two were hot after the BMW . . .'

'We lost it,' I said.

'So I see. And now you're looking for the road back.' He nodded towards the spread map. 'Follow me. We'll give you a lead.'

'Get stuffed,' said George.

'Thank you, but no,' I translated.

Williamson hesitated, then shrugged. 'The roads are gonna get bad.'

Then he got back in the patrol car, and they U-turned away.

'You weren't polite, George.'

'I got rid of him. You do the phoning. It's murder for me, getting in the box.' He looked at me in massive wonder. 'Don't you see!'

I saw. Neither of us had the change, but as George had guessed, it was not necessary. There was no reply from Collis's office.

I felt cold. We stood by the box, in the misty hollow where two deserted roads crossed. A hundred yards away, smoke rose vertically into the cold air from a squat, mournful cottage. The black clouds seemed low and the

63

snowflakes were larger. The trees melted into the sky.

'He grabbed the opportunity,' I agreed. 'But not the one you said. It all sounded wrong, George, the BMW not trying to outpace you. But the opportunity he took was when you followed it. He reported his car stolen. It placed him in his office with no car—damn it, Williamson believes he's still there—and he was free. Free, George, and God help us he could be anywhere.'

'But it wouldn't last long.' George was hunched up, his hands in his pockets, his hair white with snow. His eyes burned beneath it. 'Whatever he intended, it'd have to be quick. Reasonably.'

'It smells rotten.' There was something I should be interpreting, and it was just out of reach.

'So we should still be in time.'

'We don't know where . . .'

'We don't know where *he's* gone, but we can have a guess at where his car's gone, Dave. You said—the log house. And it'd be a big coincidence, coming this direction . . .'

Still the thought eluded me. 'It's too wild.'

'But it's all we've got. Where's that bloody map?'

A snowflake fell on Filsby, melted darkly, and gave us a solid starter. There would be no more than two miles in it, but the contour lines were close and some of it looked steep.

'I'll lead,' I said. At the worst, it would be a shortcut back to the motorway.

'Don't make it too fast. I want this car in one piece.'

I could feel the Porsche breaking away on the corners. The metalled road was winding and tricky. George, for all his weight, has a tender foot. He stuck stubbornly on my tail. I found the turnoff. Stripped logs were stacked beside an old, rusting saw bench. The Ride plunged into the trees, white against the black, protected pine needles beneath the massed firs. It looked dark in there. I put on my heads and plunged at it. The Porsche throbbed and leapt to the challenge, and still the Renault followed behind, bucking and swaying.

There could be no chance of pausing and considering. Wheelspin was getting worse as the climb grew steeper, and in places the space between the trees was tailored for clearance of no more than a Landrover. George fell behind. I eased. The track breasted a rise and for a hundred yards turned right along the brow of a level arc, black towering pines on my left, bracken down there in the hollow on my right. The wipers flung the snow sideways as it streamed back at me. I stopped, cut my engine, and listened. The whine of the Renault, rising and falling, was coming up behind.

Getting out, I could see a cut-away ahead, where the trees had been cleared. I slid back in and eased over to it, then waited for George.

He wound down the window and shouted.

'Nobody's going to come up here if he didn't have to, Dave. I'll bust the springs . . .'

'It was easier coming in the other way. It couldn't be far, now. You pull in here, and I'll try the next bend on foot.'

He watched me, his head out of the window, as I trudged on. The snow was lying an inch thick, and my shoes were soaked. When I got back, his head was still out.

'I was listening,' he said. 'It's dead out here.'

'The BMW's there.'

He looked at me.

'It's parked by the log-house,' I said.

'Why're you looking like that?'

'Adrian Collis is in it. His chest's been blasted in with a shotgun.'

He was struggling to get out. I said: 'Turn the car round and go and phone, George.'

'I want to see.'

'I can't get the Porsche past you. Get Williamson.'

He'd have walked me into the ground if I hadn't stood aside. 'You get him. I'm gonna take a look. It's me you're doubting . . .'

'No.'

'You think I'm off my head or something. I'm just going to take a look. That's all, Dave. All I want.'

'There's nothing you can do. And nobody says you're crazy.'

'I do,' he growled. 'Go and do your

phoning.'

And he stumped away.

I got the Renault back to that phone box and asked them to locate Sgt. Williamson. Then I drove back, and how George had got it up the Ride I didn't know. Twice I got stuck and had to back down and try again. The Porsche was silent and deserted when I reached it. I discovered George standing by the BMW.

'I gave 'em the map references,' I said.

'Good thinking.'

I looked at him with suspicion.

'There's a tape in the Renault,' he said dully. 'I mentioned the time when this car drove away from his office.'

'Yes George, I'm sure.'

'The call to the Station will've been logged.'

'It probably was. But it's unecessary. He described you heading off after his car.'

'Fairly accurately.'

'Don't start blaming yourself.'

He turned furiously. 'Don't you condescend to me, Dave. I can do my own reasoning.'

'All right.' I looked away. His eyes were dangerous. 'You lost the car, and it was bloody careless, and now he's dead. So go ahead and blame yourself as much as you like, you big fool.'

He walked away a few yards. The light was grey and without direction. 'I've been looking around.' Now he was quiet. 'Don't worry about footprints, the snow came after he died, and there were only yours. I wasn't thinking, Dave, not reasoning. What I really wanted to do was cry. Funny that. But not for him, mate. I felt all hot with it, because I'd had a feeling, a premonition like, and I'd expected some poor, foully-assaulted girl . . . and it was only him. I'm glad somebody did it. And now it's all over, and he's gone.'

'Is it all over? You say you weren't thinking, George. What didn't you think?'

He laughed. Steam gushed with it. 'You're slow—and I'm older than you. But I saw how it was. He took advantage? Rubbish. He *made* the opportunity. The MGB was planted there. Otherwise it's all too cosy and coincidental. A little red sports car in Plummer's slot, and Collis's car gets pinched! In a few seconds? Never. And you know it. You'd seen through it.'

I'd had the uneasy feeling, but not George's perception. 'I didn't like what we had, I'll admit that.'

He stood by the BMW. The driver's door was open, with snow on Collis's lap and on his right leg. He was sprawled in the driving seat, his head back and his face unmarked. A charge of shot had blasted into his chest, the front of his leather motoring coat black with it and torn away in a hole four inches across. The seat belt was looped over his chest, but not fastened. It was unmarked.

'He arranged it,' said George, and now his voice was toneless. 'The MGB, the taking of the BMW, and his phone call. His alibi, Dave. I know it's loose, but so are all the best alibis. Unforced and natural. He'd be pin-pointed there at the office, with his car leading me away, and be free to dive into the MGB. A fast little car, Dave. It'd take only seconds for somebody to slip from the MGB to the BMW, and drive away, with me after them.'

'And drop you casually, George? Was *that* on the programme? You're telling me he had some young girl—'

'I'm not.'

'Let me take it on logically. He'd arranged it, you say. An accomplice, who'd agreed to lead you away, then drop you . . .'

'That could've been unrehearsed.'

'. . . and then meet him here, when he arrived in the MGB. Some girl he fancied, perhaps, who'd never heard the name of Adrian Collis, rapist and murderer, and drove here happily, on a rotten February day, to be raped, and subsequently strangled, like the rest.'

'Anybody can make things sound ridiculous.' He was hot and angry.

'But it was what you expected to find.'

'Well . . .'

'Wasn't it?'

'I was pleased to find him. Anyway, it's all confirmed.'

69

'Is it? As simple as that?'

'The seat belt, Dave. Look at it. His chest blown in, and the belt untouched. He wasn't killed in this car.'

'He wasn't driving it. We know that.'

'So what're we arguing about? It all fits— the MGB gone from the car park, everything.'

I didn't know what we were arguing about. There was simply a background of illogicality about it.

'I'd just like to know who you followed in the BMW, that's all.'

I looked at what was left of Adrian Collis. I didn't know what I was feeling. I had not been convinced of his guilt; I haven't George's direct and untrammelled view of things. George makes up his own mind. I envied him.

Then, as I watched, Collis moved. I felt the skin tighten across my cheeks, although I knew it was a trick of rigor, a muscle tightening in the low temperature. Then he moved again, the head fell forward, and stiffly, as though impelled, he fell forward over the wheel.

'Not this car.' I cleared my throat. 'He died elsewhere.'

There were no bullet holes in the back of the seat squab, although the emerging shot had torn the rear of his motoring coat.

They were on their way. The sirens rose and fell in the still air, ghostly warning to the deer and other wildlife. George stirred. He looked round.

'Where the hell do they think they are—New York?'

He was angry, disturbed at the warning the sirens projected.

Fortunately, Williamson was even more angry. He had missed the possibility. It would not look good on his record.

He was so angry that he omitted to search our cars.

CHAPTER FIVE

It was days before I could get the chill out of my bones. We stood around and waited. Williamson and his mates searched the area and swarmed around the car, and later a Superintendent called Thwaites appeared, and seemed to do nothing but eye us with suspicion. We each made statements, and when they finally released us it had been dark for two hours. Walking away from that headlight-swept clearing, we were temporarily blinded.

George wasn't saying anything. The trip back down to the road was going to be tricky, but he didn't seem to hear my warning. Before I'd manoeuvred the Porsche round, he'd gone in a cloud of exhaust steam.

I caught him in the public bar of the Crown. He didn't seem to be as hungry as I was, except perhaps for warmth and companionship —and congratulations.

The news had preceded us. You know how these things flare across space like a forest fire. It was known that Adrian Collis had been removed from public danger. It was also known that George and I were the ones who had failed in our duties and allowed that to happen. They were buying George a drink.

Sometimes you can't tell with George. Generally speaking he is open and obvious, but sometimes his face becomes set, only experience tells you that he's close to an explosion.

I tried to get between them. 'Let's go and eat, George.'

He looked at me, and through me. 'There's a drink for you, too.'

'No, no. I did very little.'

'True. All my own work. But drink it down, Dave.'

'What I need's a brandy.'

'A brandy for my friend!'

There was enough expression in his voice, now, to moderate the excited chatter around us. It tailed off into a murmuring uneasiness.

I took my drink. It washed me with a temporary warmth, but the basic chill quelled it.

'Aren't you going to pack?' I asked casually.

'I'm not going anywhere.'

'What's there to stay for? Our man's dead.

Surely you can't expect paying for it. You go home, George. Leave the nasty bit to me.'

'I thought we'd had that.'

'There's Mrs. Collis to see.'

Slowly the chatter had grown again, with its centre moved away from us. It only takes a touch of reality to burst a bubble of hysteria. I waited for George's eyes to soften. The mention of Delia worked.

'Williamson said he'd go.'

'That makes it easy. So there's nothing to keep us here.'

He looked away and grabbed at his glass. 'I'd just like to meet him and shake his hand.'

'Who's that then?'

'This public hero, the one that did him in.'

I laughed. 'You think he'll stand up and be counted?'

'In here, why not! He's amongst friends.' Then he peered over the edge of his glass, slowly turning his head, eyeing each one in turn. 'If he's here, and if he's got the guts,' he said flatly.

It could have been that easy. Somewhere there was a pillar of the community who had deprived it of Collis's company. It was a heady time for him. The temptation would be enormous. There's many a murderer who's confessed because his accomplishment remains hidden.

There was a shuffle. The crowd parted to reveal Reuben Goldwater, half cowering, trying to grin, looking round in appeal.

'Oh no,' he whispered, and the tension dissolved in a roar of laughter.

'Aren't we going to eat now?' I asked.

'You eat if you want to. Me, I'm going out. Delia Collis is going to be very frightened and very lonely.'

'So you're going to comfort her?'

'I'm going to fetch her sister.'

Naturally, I went with him. We took a fistful of sandwiches and the Renault, in case we had to run Amanda over to her sister's. George was quiet. The car ran well, apart from a strange hum. Then I realised it was George.

'What you so cheerful about?'

'Who said I'm cheerful? All right, cheerful then. It's been lousy for me, Dave, these last few days.'

'I haven't been so happy myself.'

'You know what I mean. You were fine. You've got a do-gooder streak in you. You're the sort that thinks everybody's innocent once you can understand 'em, how they tick and what makes their wheels go round. Then you can excuse them.'

'Understanding isn't excusing.'

'Come off it. You just sat back, all warm and happy. You told yourself there was just a chance he hadn't done those three murders. It made it easy for you.'

'But you, George—'

'I hadn't finished.'

'You had, mate. Your bit. Now it's my turn. You, George, were just as convinced he had done 'em. And that made it easy for you. Watch the road, blast you. All you'd got to think was that somehow—if any girl was in danger—you'd got to be there, because Collis would be. And this time you'd get him. No, George, it's you who's had it easy. It's now that things are going to get difficult.'

'Now . . . what?'

'Because it isn't going to finish with comforting Delia Collis and walking away. This partnership's suffered enough. First we protect a convicted murderer. Then we fail to protect him. Now . . . how'll it look if we just walk away from it? And make no mistake, George, you're not going to split us up. That'd be the end of our reputation. And I intend to stay here and dig out who did it.'

'I don't care who did it.'

'I know you don't. That's why it's going to be difficult for you.'

'If you think I'm—'

'I do think it. Now shut up and let me concentrate.'

'What's there to concentrate about?'

'I'll think of something.'

And ten minutes later, I had. I roused.

'Collis wouldn't do all that wangling with cars in order to meet somebody who hated him.'

'You work it out, Dave. Me . . . I'm driving.'

75

'So, if one of 'em did it—his enemies—then you've got to ask yourself how they knew where to go to wait for Collis.'

'I don't have to ask myself anything.'

'As you wish, George. Any idea where we're going?'

'Flat 27, Riverside Court. You put it on tape.'

'So I did. Don't you have to look at a street map?'

His fingers stroked the wheel. We took a fast bend with stability. There had been little snow here.

'I looked it up,' he said, and I glanced at him with curiosity.

You couldn't be sure if they were council flats or privately owned. Nowadays they're building a quality of impersonality into everything, presenting a puzzle for future historians to type the seventies style. This architect had shied away from high-rise, and gently avoided a suggestion of uniformity. The block had the contours of a destroyer, all ups and downs and purposeful curves.

Flat 27 was a ground floor one, where the building curtsied and swerved to avoid an oval of greenery and landscaping in concrete. Until my finger was actually on the button I had assumed that Amanda Greaves had been told. George stood at my side, his head thrown back.

'Who's going to tell her?' he asked, and the

76

door opened.

She was in slacks and a polo-necked jumper and wearing no make-up. As it should always be, I thought, with those marvellous eyes, which closed and opened again, and blurred as she whispered:

'What's happened?'

I glanced round. 'Well . . .'

'Come in. Do come in. I knew it, I just knew it. Oh, don't tell me there's another . . .'

So it wasn't going to be such a shock. 'No, Miss Greaves, it's not another girl. It's Adrian Collis himself. I'm sorry. He's dead.'

She caught her lower lip in her teeth. 'Oh dear God! How?'

'It isn't very pleasant.'

She flashed her eyes at me. 'You were supposed to be protecting Adrian. You let those morons get at him.'

'One only, I think.' We were still in the hall. 'One person—moron or otherwise—reached him with a shotgun.' Her breath was indrawn quickly. 'It would have been quite sudden.'

'Thank you for coming to tell me.' She gave an awkward little wave with one hand.

'It wasn't why we came. Your sister . . .'

'Poor Delia. How is she taking it?'

'We haven't seen her. We just thought you'd want to be with her.'

Her little laugh was choked, biting. 'Quite obviously you haven't seen her. She'd have said she didn't want me.'

'You've quarrelled then?'

'Nothing . . . oh dear, no. Nothing new. It's always been the same. She resents me, and always has. I'm the elder. I suppose I'm bossy. Do I give you that impression? I see I do. But she was always foolish and stubborn. I've had to lead her and guide her, and advise her. But when we came to this . . .'

'Came to what?'

'How she insisted on staying with him . . . I pleaded with her, but this time . . .' She threw up her hands in supplication. 'Nothing would budge her. Not the danger—and she *was* in danger there, you can't deny it. But no. I'm married to him, she said, as though somebody had chained them together.'

George had been silent all this time. But now he spoke. George, the bachelor, rumbled warningly: 'Some people take it seriously.'

She looked at him. I read her thought: Ye Gods, what've we got here? She smiled sourly. 'I'd understand if she loved him, because then she could be blind to it all and forgive it.'

'All, Miss Greaves?' I asked.

'This business. You know! But it was all gone, whatever she'd felt for him. Oh, she didn't fool me. It was sheer stupid loyalty.'

'Very disturbing,' I said comfortingly. 'We've got a car outside.'

'Do you really think I could go to her?'

'If you tried not to say you told her so, and that you knew he'd come to a sticky end . . .

yes. I think you could go, and even find her grateful.'

She raised her chin. Her voice was sharp. 'If I did decide to go, it'd be in my own car.'

'Luxury car at your service,' George cut in, his voice so mocking that I knew she'd have to take him up.

'You're a fool if you don't realise I'd have to get back here.'

'Oh, but we'll be around,' he said. 'Quite a while, I reckon.'

'What is he saying?'

I explained to her. 'I've persuaded him to stay with me. I'll have to find out who killed him, now won't I?'

'If it gives you satisfaction.'

'For everybody's satisfaction.'

Her eyes were blank as she turned from us, and we didn't get to see the flat. Not that time, anyway.

'I don't know how you do it,' said George, as we got in the Renault. 'You create situations, and now we've got no alternative.'

'I've realised that. She's only got to give herself enough time for self-justification, and nothing'll keep her away from Delia. So we've got to go and warn her.'

'I knew you'd say that.' He sighed, with resignation, I thought.

But things went wrong that night, all round. The bungalow was empty and dark when we arrived. Rattling the gate didn't raise any

79

protest from Major, so it meant that Delia had him with her. Ten to one at the Station, and for heaven knew how long.

Just to make sure, we climbed the gate and went to ring the bell, in case she was weeping in the dark, but all that happened was that a fat, sleek grey cat rubbed himself against our legs. Major's alleged meal was emerging in the dog's absence.

All was peaceful and quiet. It was as though the whole district had sighed with relief at Collis's passing. The trees across the road stood straight and calmly dignified under their coating of snow, and the rustlings were innocent and wild.

But you see how it left us. We had Amanda no doubt heading there, so we couldn't just leave her to find the place empty. So we waited, half the night through, and it did not occur to either of us that she'd use her intelligence and phone before she left the flat. It did occur to us to phone the flat ourselves, and I walked along the road until I found a box, but there was no reply from Flat 27. Which was what put us off.

Nevertheless, neither Delia nor Amanda arrived while we were there, and when we got back to town, getting on for two in the morning, we'd missed all the excitement.

The evidence was still there in the bar. The lights were on and they were clearing up the mess. The police had come to collect Reuben

Goldwater and his belligerent friend, Jonas Fletcher. They had arrived at a poorly-chosen time, when the bar was packed with well-wishers, who might not have proof that either of them had killed Collis, but were sufficiently drunk to wish themselves into believing that one of them had.

It had taken half an hour for the police to winkle out their two witnesses—and that would have been only for questioning.

Andy Partridge, we heard the following morning, had made a show of it for the public record, and had been chased across three counties before he took a corner too fast for two wheels. There had been no injury to vehicle or rider, except perhaps to his pride.

Mind you, he'd probably recover his pride when he discovered that they actually thought him capable of murder.

CHAPTER SIX

Sgt. Williamson joined us for breakfast. That's to say, he sat with us while we ate, and emptied our teapot.

'The Super's intrigued,' he said. 'Pass the sugar, will you.'

George and I chewed.

'It's your part in this affair,' he went on. 'You do see why, I'm sure. There's been a most strange and garbled story from his wife, but of course it can't be true. Tell me it's not true.'

George looked at me. We did not speak.

'Something about being around when the next girl was attacked. He can't have hired you for such a thing, to be there when he actually did it.'

He poured his second cup. I cleared my throat, and he looked expectant. George said:

'Have you found the weapon?'

'You're not being co-operative. Now me— I've never seen any point in hiding things. So I'll tell you. No, we haven't found any weapon. As I was saying, if that was your idea, to catch him in the act, so to speak, how'd you come to let him get away? No . . . I've heard the story— sorry, your evidence.' He laughed, stirring vigorously. 'What I meant was that we can understand you'd want to let him *think* he was slipping you. But how the hell did you come to bungle it so . . . well, so stupidly?'

George reached for the pot a second too late. 'Any footprints?' he asked with interest, his hand in the air.

'After you two—what d'you expect?'

'But the weather forecast says milder,' I pointed out. 'When the snow melts, it could reveal something.'

'When're you leaving?' Williamson asked. 'You'll have to let us know.'

'We're going up to see Delia Collis,' George

said. 'I take it she's home now?'

'Her sister came to the Station. There was a scene. The Super sent them both away. Oh dear, there's no more tea.'

I watched him leave, wondering what he'd been fishing for. 'Did you mean that, about going to see Delia?'

'Not at the time I said it. But I'd love to hear about that scene. Let's go ask her.'

I wondered what George was fishing for, too, but I went along with what he wanted to do.

The gate was wide open, with Major lolling his tongue at us just inside. Two cars stood in the drive, Amanda's Morris Minor and a Mini, which I assumed to be Delia's.

Amanda let us in. She had taken control. There was an aura of protectiveness about the place.

'How you've got the nerve to come here, after what's happened . . .'

'Is she resting?' I asked.

'Resting be damned. She's sorting out her recordings.'

Anything to keep the hands busy and the mind occupied, I decided. Delia was in the long room, wearing a nylon housecoat.

'Good of you to come,' she said politely. Her gaze wandered from me, sought out a vase, and she went to adjust its position. Amanda took it from her, shooing her to a seat.

'Have you had breakfast?' Delia asked. She was smoothing, over and over, the surface of the housecoat across her knees.

'Breakfast . . . but no tea.'

'I'm sure Amanda would only be too pleased . . .' The sentence faded away as she met Amanda's gaze.

'We'd like that,' George said.

'Dying for a cup,' I agreed.

Amanda left the room with long, tense strides. Delia stared at a far corner of the room.

'I shall go quite insane if she stays here another hour,' she murmured.

'We thought you'd like company.' I glanced at George, who was impassive. 'Perhaps we made a mistake.'

'I'd like to be alone. There's really no danger, now. I shall insist. It's my home . . . I *can* insist?' She looked the question at me.

'Legally, yes. What was the upset at the Station?'

Her hands fluttered; her lips tried to smile. 'She insisted that they must release me. It was embarrassing because they were being so kind. They were not *holding* me, you understand.'

'But for a long while,' I pointed out. 'Why were they so dissatisfied, I wonder?'

'It's so strange. Adrian . . .' She used the name casually; just somebody she used to know. 'Adrian went to that place, so who could have known where to find him? As simple as

84

that.'

Amanda clattered a tray in, deliberately dispersing the intimacy. I waited for the atmosphere to settle. Amanda sat and poured tea. George sat opposite her, but I walked my cup around.

'There's the person he arranged to meet,' I suggested at last.

'They do not seem to believe that.'

George moved. I flashed him a warning, and he relaxed.

'What do they believe?'

Delia shook her head. 'I don't really understand. Something about one of you . . .'

'It was me,' said George shortly.

'Whoever it was, they seem to believe there's . . . what did he call it . . . a cover-up. They believe that Adrian simply drove there. That there wasn't anybody he was meeting.'

'I will *not* have you upset,' Amanda burst out. 'Really, Delia, this is absurd. You should be resting.'

'And you, my dear, should be at work.'

I put down my empty cup. 'Then before Miss Greaves has to go—while you're both together—there's just one thing I'd like to ask.' I smiled from one to the other, Delia listless but making an effort, Amanda brittle. 'You're the two who were closest to him. I'm not talking about evidence now, but of atmosphere and instinct—intuition, if you like. Did Adrian kill those three girls?'

85

There was a gasp from Amanda. George grunted in protest, as though I had punched him. Amanda said:

'How dare you! At a time like this.'

'At a time like this you're more likely to admit the truth to yourselves.'

Delia lifted her head. 'I suppose he did. Does it matter?'

Amanda was shocked. 'How you can calmly say such a thing . . .'

'And you?' I asked. 'What was your opinion, Miss Greaves?'

'Adrian could never, in all this world, do such a thing!' She caught her lower lip in her teeth, then clasped her hands to her face before it could crumple away. She shook her head desperately, driving it from her. One hand sought Delia's.

'You mean yes?' I asked gently.

'Yes, yes,' she whispered bitterly. 'Oh Delia! My dear, my dear! I knew, and I suffered, seeing you here with him, and not getting away.'

Delia looked at us. Her face was drawn, but she had a quiet, deep courage, much more solidly planted and experienced than her sister's.

'You've upset her now. Poor Amanda, you should go home. And rest.'

'Of course she should,' I agreed, and between us, George and I, we managed to get Amanda into her sheepskin coat, into her car, and on the road before she'd recovered her equanimity.

'I can't thank you both enough,' said Delia ambiguously, 'for what you've done.'

She was standing in the open front door at the time, gazing after her sister. Her eyes were cold.

We were using the Renault again, and George got us well clear before he burst out with what I'd been expecting.

'What the hell did Thwaites mean by that—there's been a cover-up!'

'Oh come on, George. You can't imagine he'd tell a witness what he thought could have happened. No. That was Delia's idea. Somehow she's got to believe that. I wonder why.'

'You're crafty. You never let on. What were you up to, in there?'

'Me?'

'Springing that on them.'

'It helped to know, I thought, who's really the dominant one.'

'That poor Delia, treating her like that!'

'I know, George. Where're you heading?'

'For his offices. Where else?'

'Then you see why I said it. I had to get you going, somehow.'

I laughed. After a minute, George laughed, too. But there was no heart in it.

'It's all we've got, Dave,' he explained, as though I hadn't realised it. 'Collis had it all fixed with some accomplice or other, and that accomplice brought along the MGB, and parked it in Plummer's slot.'

'I'm with you.'

We left the car in the street outside Collis's office, and got out to walk the last bit.

'They swapped cars, in effect, while I was round the other side of the car park. There, Dave, over there in the far corner, that's where I was when the BMW drove away. Then Collis phoned the police, to give himself an alibi, and he'd got the MGB and a clear run.'

'We don't know it was anything but a distraction for us,' I pointed out. 'We *don't* know that there was any intention for those two to meet again. It's likely he only wanted to give himself a free run at the female population.'

'So now you're accepting it.' George was derisory.

'I'm accepting the possibility. Trying to see all round it. Maybe the log house was his usual base for his activities, and there was no intention of meeting that accomplice there.'

'But they did meet, because the BMW was there, and Collis was shot. So the accomplice is the one we've got to find.'

'The only clue is the MGB.'

I was watching him, slightly amused. Last night, definite opposition. Now, all of a sudden, enthusiasm.

'You tell me, George.'

88

'It's unlikely it'd actually belong to the accomplice. That would be too risky, and seeing the sort of car it was, ideal for his purpose, it was . . .'

'Ideal for who's purpose, George?'

'Collis's of course.'

'So you're saying there was a definite intention of a fast run somewhere? To the log house, then? By major roads, seeing that the accomplice took the motorway.'

'Who's telling this, anyway?'

'You are, George. I was just exercising your ego a bit.'

'I was *going* to say that the MGB was obviously hired because of what it was, to leave for Collis's use. We don't know what coercion he might have used. But you see how it is—all we've got to do is find the hire firm and ask who hired it.'

'And who returned it?'

'Is that likely, Dave? Use your loaf. Who hired it'll be enough.'

'All of which should be dead easy. Not many hire firms have sports cars on their books.'

We had to go Birmingham to find it, and that was on the advice of the nearest Avis. This was a specialist hire firm—the odd Daimler or Jensen for that special effect you wished to create; the few snappy sports jobs to impress the girls. Yes, they had a red MGB out on hire. Of course they would look it up—anything for the city C.I.D. George looked innocent and

89

very official.

The man fetched his books. You have to produce a driving licence to hire a car, so we expected a decent lead.

The car had been hired, with a huge deposit, by Adrian Palmer Collis.

George said not a word, but turned on his heel and went out to the Renault. He came back with a sketch of Wolverhampton's deplorable horse—one of Collis's subtler clues which was signed A. P. Collis. The signatures matched. The one on the hire contract was written above the date. It was thirteen days before.

We returned to the Renault. George did not immediately drive away. He grasped the steering wheel firmly, and stared ahead.

'Before he engaged us,' I said.

'He'd got it all planned.'

'Car first, then the less important details, such as the two idiots to give him an alibi.'

'When he was good and ready, Dave. When it suited him to go out and do whatever he wanted to do.'

'People don't plan sex assaults thirteen days ahead.'

'But they plan murders.'

'The accomplice, George? Is that who you mean? Lured to the log house on some pretence, and then to be killed.'

'It leaves us no lead at all. Just a red MGB, abandoned somewhere.'

'So think, George. Go on, do your memory trick. That MGB. Visualise it, man. There must have been somebody sitting in it, in the car park, as you drove past.'

'It doesn't follow.'

'But visualise it.'

'I'm doing that. Don't push me, Dave.'

'A low, red car . . .'

'I know what it looks like. For God's sake, shut up a bit.'

'Just trying to help.'

I sat and sulked for three minutes. Then at last:

'Somebody *could* have been in it, and I wouldn't see.'

'Why not, George?'

'Because the visor was down.'

'Perhaps so that you wouldn't see.'

'But the sun was low. The snow hadn't started. You weren't even awake, but first thing yesterday morning the east was clear sky. The visor could've been down because the car'd been driven in from the west. Collis hired it thirteen days ago. He'd have to leave it somewhere the police wouldn't pick it up, a long-stay car park, say. Dave . . . a long-stay car park to the west, not too far away . . . The Airport, Dave!'

'Good thinking.'

He looked at me suspiciously. I said: 'Let's go and have a look, then.'

The motorway is almost due west to east,

91

which made the car park at the Airport a pretty wild guess. There were a thousand alternatives, but it was where I'd choose to dump a car.

You drive in and take a ticket. As you drive out, a man at the barrier checks the time and date and asks you for a lot of money. The previous morning he must have collected twelve days' parking fee on the red MGB. It was odds against his remembering.

'Twelve days is a funny period,' the old fellow said. 'Mid-winter, too, it's the ski-ing crowd. Ten days or a fortnight, but never twelve. That's why I remember.'

'You do?'

'Drives out with this little sports car and pays £24.20. By dinner time, drives out again and pays five hours on a scruffy old saloon. Sure I remember.'

'Scruffy old saloon?'

'A Morris Minor. There's still some about.'

'Can you describe her?'

'You knew,' he accused me. 'I didn't say it was a woman.' He went on to describe Amanda Greaves.

We drove on into the parking area. It was divided into huge compounds: long stay, short stay, and don't know till I get back. The little red MGB was in the short stay. Amanda had had to return for her own car.

'It's too easy,' said George suspiciously.

We stood and looked at the car. We were

92

both wearing driving gloves. I tried the door. It had been left open, keys on the passenger's seat. I peered in, disturbing nothing.

'This is the car,' I said.

'I'd guessed that.'

'Proof though, now. There're shotgun pellet holes in the driver's seat squab. And what looks like blood.'

We walked back to the Renault. Our short stay cost 20p. George was morose.

'I wonder,' he said at last, 'what it'd take to sit in that seat, with his blood in the small of your back.'

'It was something she'd have to do. We'd better phone the police.'

'There's a box right in front of Riverside Court.'

'That's twenty-seven miles from here, George,' I said gently.

He eased the Renault onto the road and headed for the motorway junction.

'We wouldn't want the police to get her first, Dave, now would we.'

George wouldn't, anyway.

CHAPTER SEVEN

We had not parted amicably, so it was not surprising when Amanda tried to slam the door in our faces. George reached past me and

rested a hand against the door, and that was
that. She turned away in exasperation and
allowed us to follow her.

The previous time, we had seen only the
hall. When we walked into the flat she was
standing, half turned away, lighting a cigarette
nervously. She had venetian blinds at the
window, and these were nearly closed. The
room was dim. She had a gas fire going, and
there was an eerie glow to the whitewood
furniture. None of the chairs looked as though
it would support George.

She spoke bitterly. 'You sent me off home
to rest, but you won't allow me to.' Her voice
was harsh. 'Put the light on, if you must.'

That was simply to indicate that she had
nothing to fear from the light. But when
George put it on, there was. Her eyes looked
bruised, and the shock was still flooding them.

She raised her chin. 'I don't usually give
way,' she claimed.

'I'm surprised,' I admitted. 'I'd have
thought, being such an emotional woman . . .
But perhaps not, seeing how things were.'

'What does that mean?'

'Practice. It must have been going on a long
time. You'd need every bit of restraint you
could lay your hands on in order to carry on.
And resolution.'

She was looking at me, the cigarette
smouldering in her fingers, her eyes narrowed,
perhaps against the smoke.

94

'We've just come from the Airport, Miss Greaves. We were looking at a small, red MGB, which had been hired thirteen days ago by Adrian Collis. There's evidence that he was killed while he was sitting behind the wheel, and the description we have seems to indicate that you drove it for him to his office, and left in his BMW. Tell me if this is all fantasy, because we'd like to hear it's not true.'

'But I'm proud of it. Proud!'

'You're making things very easy.'

'I'm glad to hear something's easy for somebody. Believe me, there's been nothing easy in *my* life. Not ever.'

I glanced at George, but he was unresponsive. Leave it to Dave, that seemed to be what he implied.

'I think you've perhaps taken your responsibilities too seriously,' I suggested.

Her voice was scathing. 'Are you talking about the same thing?'

'I'm talking about your relationship with your sister, protecting her, as you thought, from the harsh facts of life. I can well imagine that when you began to feel some attraction for Adrian Collis, and when it grew, and when he responded, then you'd want to protect her from that, too.'

'Men are very simple. I don't know how half of you get through life—you've got no imagination. Do you think I cared for Delia? It was Adrian . . . Adrian! It was he who would suffer. The poor damned idiot, he still felt something for her. He said he couldn't leave her . . . how much he'd hate to hurt her feelings. How much it'd hurt him! That tells you what an idiot I was. Any other woman would have thrown him out on his ear. But I loved him. There was nothing I would not have done . . . Oh, what's the use of talking to you. You can't understand. You wouldn't know.'

'Perhaps I do. You're speaking with contempt, so I can understand, at least, that you'd have the same contempt for Delia.'

She stared at me. 'You're a fool.'

'You say that because you think I admire her. Perhaps I do. She's very courageous.'

Her laugh was brittle. 'The little fool, she didn't know what she had in Adrian . . . his loyalty. She rejected him.'

'Rejected?'

'She was his wife!' Amanda cried. 'That was the be-all and end-all of it. A contract which they'd signed. An oath they'd sworn. To have and to hold. She let it go that far. He had her and she held him, but dear God her hands must have been cold. The letter of the contract, but not the warmth. Isn't *that* rejecting? Haven't you ever realised, it's men who framed the marriage vows. For men. They didn't realise they were storing up distress for themselves. People like Delia are too literal. I bet she's cherished every word. For better or worse! She *enjoyed* the worse bit, when it came. She could bask in it. I'm his wife! She screamed it at you without saying a word. Let no man put asunder! But oh dear Lord, that man was Adrian, and he couldn't throw it back in her face. He just couldn't.'

'However much you pleaded with him.'

'I did not, damn you. I loved him. *I* cherished him.'

'Why don't you sit down?'

'Because I prefer to stand. If you're going to fling accusations at me, I can stand on my own two feet.'

'Of what did you expect to be accused?'

'Whatever the legal phrase is. I'm sure there must be one. I went along with what he wanted me to do—because I loved him. I picked up the MGB for him, and did just what he told me to.'

'Including dropping my partner when he followed you?'

She glanced at George. 'It was so simple, and it worked just as Adrian said it would. We had to meet secretly, because we could not meet any other way, and because . . .' She shook her head, dismissing it, but the pain was in the line of her jaw.

'And because of what?'

She stared directly into my eyes. 'Because he intended to kill me.'

I allowed the idea to penetrate and develop. Then at last:

'I don't understand.'

'Didn't I say you wouldn't!' she snapped. 'I don't know why we're wasting time, talking like this . . .'

'It's not a waste. Very soon you're going to be saying much the same thing to the police, and it's likely that they'll understand even less. So treat this as a dress rehearsal.'

'It's not bloody play-acting.'

'A dummy run, then, if you prefer that. Tell us why he wished to murder you—or at least why you'd think so.'

I was trying to choose my words carefully. She was in an unstable emotional condition and I didn't want it to overflow into hysteria, when nothing she said would be valid. I wasn't too sure of what she'd already said. George was looking unimpressed.

She sighed, the heart going out of her. For one moment she had thought she'd met someone who might understand.

'The facts?' she asked flatly. 'Just the bare facts, is that what you want?'

'If you'll try not to confuse us.'

'Then you'll need to realise that I knew Adrian before he married my sister. My work . . . I could put him in the way of business. I didn't expect gratitude. At the wedding, he put his arm around me and said how much he owed me for bringing them together! Wasn't that splendid of him. But I watched it go stale, all that bright face of happiness sliding away. We met casually, then more often, and then he began to come here. His job took him away, with his times of return flexible. He would stay with me. Sometimes the whole night—what he called a stopover. I gave him what Delia denied him, perhaps even then not enough.'

She paused, waiting for a comment. I merely inclined my head.

'When . . . that terrible thing happened, I was quite insane with it all pouring over me. It was as though I was drowning. They arrested him for rape and murder. He came here, one last time. He seemed to know he was going to be arrested. There was the question of alibis, you see. He refused to let me testify for him.'

'You could have sworn he was here, all three times?'

'Now you're really being stupid.' Restlessly she moved, touching things she knew and loved. 'How could I be so certain? There were no crosses on my calendar. But I could have explained why he had no alibis.'

'But again he refused to hurt Delia?'

'That was the way he put it.' The words were barely articulate. 'I could have killed him. But he refused, flatly.'

'You don't strike me as a person who would accept that.'

'His wishes . . .'

'You'd just stand aside and watch him go through that? Even watch him sentenced!'

'If you're not going to believe what I say . . .'

99

'I'm trying to understand.'

'I'm giving you the facts. He was tried, as you say, and sentenced, and the life went clear out of me. But then the miracle happened. He was released. I knew he would come back to me. But he didn't. It was as though the past was dead.'

'But I can't see why you'd fear him.'

She looked vague, sliding round it. 'Fact,' she claimed. 'He hated me. You're a man. You work it out. But he *did* want to see me— once—oh what a treat! One last time. Fond farewells. It was a complicated set-up, but you know that, and all I'd got to wait for was the go-ahead by post, and the place we were to meet.'

'You got that by post? Yesterday morning?'

'Yes.'

'And had to collect the MGB, get back to the office . . .'

'My post arrives before half past seven. There was time to get back and switch to his BMW. I drove to the log house, but he had a fast car, and though he started later he got there first. When I arrived he was dead in the MGB.'

'Ah!'

'You don't believe that!'

'You're saying you moved his dead body from one car to the other. A difficult job.' She was nodding, barely lifting her head, her eyes on me from beneath her brows, hunted, wary.

'But you're a strong young woman, and you were desperate, because you had to get the MGB back to the Airport and recover your own car. Am I right?'

'You're very clever, when it's all obvious.'

'And there would be blood on your clothes, all over you. A mess.'

She shuddered. 'There are no open fires here, and no furnace. I took them in a suitcase, after you called last night, and dumped them . . . But why should I say where?'

'Why indeed? You returned the MGB. Locked it up . . .'

'A weak trap. No, I left it open, the keys on the driver's seat.' I nodded. 'And drove home. Why are you playing with detail?'

'Trying to separate the truths from the half-truths.'

Her hair swirled. 'Every word has been true.'

'I'm not satisfied about your explanation of why you could not give evidence for him.'

'Because he wished . . . *you're* not satisfied! Who the hell d'you think you are to question me?'

'I'm the one who doesn't understand why, if you loved him, you would not go to the police with his alibi—for Adrian, mind you, and to hell with Delia's feelings.'

'They would not have believed me.'

'You say he came to you, on those three nights?'

101

'I did not say that. I didn't keep records.'

'But you wouldn't need to. A man does a thing like that . . . he doesn't come away from it calm and unruffled. Not immaculate, with no blood on his clothes, not a crease anywhere.'

She whispered: 'There was no blood. The reports said that.'

'I'm trying to accept what you've told me. You said he intended to kill you. You've given no reason. All you've given me is one tiny, meagre clue.'

'This is ridiculous.' But her eyes were hunting.

'You said you gave him what your sister had failed to—but even then it was perhaps not enough. You were thinking of those three girls. He would need to go somewhere, afterwards. Not to his wife. They can't face their wives. It would be natural for him to come here.'

'You're putting words in my mouth.'

'But it would be natural?'

'If he had done those . . . those things, I suppose it . . .' She couldn't complete it.

'Yet you've already said you believed he had done them.'

'I denied it!'

'You rejected it, but it was there. You didn't simply believe he had done them, you knew. You knew because he came here afterwards, each time, and you calmed him and comforted him and tidied him, before you sent him home to Delia.'

I had almost forgotten George. He broke in easily.

'I don't think you need to flog it, Dave.'

I stared at him. I was that far from an admission. She was jerking her head violently, moaning, 'no, no, no.' It was the sort of denial that crumples down to yes.

'But I do,' I insisted. 'It's the reason she couldn't give evidence for him. Because, with the least bit of cross-examination, it'd change to evidence against him. She didn't dare, George. Didn't dare.'

'You get so excited, Dave. We get the point. Nobody's disputing it. Now, you see, you've upset her. You just sit down, love, and take it easy. My friend's a bit slow, so I'll do all the explaining. Dave, it's the reason why she thought he intended to kill her. She was the only one who *knew.* Oh sure, you'll say it didn't matter any more—but it did. He'd got his way to make in the world, and he'd only be able to do it if he was shown to be innocent. You can't deny that. So he cooked up this scheme. Two mugs to give him an alibi, and the lamb not only coming to the slaughter, but actually assisting.'

I didn't know what George was doing. He'd gone all soft and considerate. Amanda was sitting, staring at nothing.

'And there he'd be,' said George expansively, 'if he pulled it off, with an alibi to a murder

103

that'd look like the fourth of a series . . . because he could even make it look like another rape.' He gave one of his ghastly laughs; my scalp tingled. 'She might even help him in that, seeing how long they'd been separated. And then where'd he be? Beautifully and manifestly innocent of all four.'

'What are you trying to do, George?' I asked softly.

'I'm showing that she'd have a damn good reason to expect him to kill her.'

'She said that, though I could hardly believe it.'

'But Dave,' he cried, slapping my shoulder, 'it would explain why she'd go there armed.' And I understood the light in his eye.

Then she moved. In a second she had her back against a sideboard, her arms spread on its surface behind her.

'I didn't say that!'

'Of course you didn't, dear,' said George gently.

'I found him dead.'

'Why deny it? Self-defence, when a triple murderer's involved? Who's going to blame you? What you knew was dangerous to him, and you realised it. He'd changed, and you knew that, too. So you'd naturally go armed.'

She fumbled with one of the drawers. She was awkwardly placed, her back to it, and the drawer stuck. With a whimper she turned and dragged the drawer open, turned back, and George ambled towards her.

'There,' he murmured. 'You see. That's what I meant.'

She was pointing a neat little .22 automatic at his chest, at a range close enough to sting badly, if not actually to draw blood.

George took it from her. 'You must never,' he said, 'never point a pistol at anybody unless you intend to use it.'

'I would've killed you.'

'Not with this.' He grinned and tossed it to me.

It was a genuine pistol, and, as far as I could detect, loaded. But it was so far gone in decrepitation that it could not possibly have fired. The fine tooling was scarred with rust, and the safety catch rusted on solid.

'You see what I mean,' said George.

'I see nothing.'

'She *had* to go armed. If she hadn't produced that piffling thing, we'd have had to wonder what it was she did take.'

He was bland, his smile radiant. He was a great, blundering problem to me, determined to stand in the way of any solution that appeared. He didn't want anybody arrested for Adrian's murder.

'The police'll wonder that. They'll talk about shotguns, George, not piddling little pistols.'

He was magnificent in triumph. 'Then tell

105

me how she could have had such a shotgun, Dave, up at the log house. She had to collect the MGB. If she had one with her then, there would be no time to get to the log house, or anywhere near there, and plant it. So, if she had one with her, in the MGB, she'd have to transfer it to the BMW. But how? It'd have to be right under Adrian Collis's nose. It is just not feasible, Dave.'

'You're making a friend for life.' I glanced at her. She was looking down at her hands.

'I can't help it. It's my personality. Miss Greaves, I wish you'd sit down again. We're not going to rush off to the police, but I'm sure they'll find their way here. So you just have a nice, quiet sit, and get your story straight for them.'

'It is *not* a story.'

'Statement, then. You'll find they're very sympathetic. Come on, Dave, there's work to do.'

Wondering, I followed him out.

'What the devil was that all about, George?'

He was placid. 'She didn't do it.'

'You big fool! That shotgun theory won't wash with the police. She could've left it in the MGB, behind the seats, been waiting for him when he drove up, and when he opened the door, reached behind for the gun and blasted him.'

He beamed. 'That's just the point, Dave. If she'd left the gun in the MGB, she'd *have* to have been waiting for him, meeting him as he drove up. Otherwise, she couldn't guarantee another chance of getting at it. But if that'd been the case she'd have driven like mad to get there first, not fiddled around like she did.' He drew himself up. 'I'm happy he's dead, and leave it at that.'

'Leave it at that! You're going to tell Thwaites that *you're* happy to leave it at that?'

'You can do it, Dave.'

'You wanted to come here, and get here before the police. You as good as said that. He'll eat our ears off.'

'You talk to him. You're good at it. We came to see her because we knew she couldn't have done it.'

I got in the car, slamming the door. He was a moment or two following me. I was still furious. I was gentle with him.

'So she told us the truth, George! That little pantomime with the pistol she said she took with her . . . oh, that was very real. Only she had all night to work it out. But go on. You believe her, if you want to. Any female who looks at you with big eyes could have you for tea. But just tell me, George, if you're so damned clever, what we're left with. If *she* didn't do it, it's got to be a third party. And if their meeting was so hell-fired secret, how could any other person have possibly known where to find the place?'

I had him there. He simply said nothing as

he started the engine. But he did not drive away, simply sat there. Then at last:

'I don't know how—but there was a third party.'

'Nonsense.'

'You heard her say distinctly that she left the MGB with the keys on the driver's seat.'

'So she said.'

'When we found it, the keys were on the passenger's seat. Tell me how that could've happened, unless somebody followed the MGB from the log house and actually got in behind the wheel after she had left it.'

I sighed. It's no good arguing with George.

When I looked across at the flat. I saw the venetian blinds snap open.

'We'd better phone Thwaites,' I said.

CHAPTER EIGHT

We got back to the Crown, and Sgt. Williamson was waiting in the lounge with half his pint left and a message for us.

'The Super wants to see you.'

'And about time, too,' said George heartily. 'Lord, this detecting makes you hungry. I wonder what our landlord can find for us.'

Williamson ordered a re-fill. 'He said now.'

'How could he have said now?' George demanded. 'When he said it, he couldn't have known when now would be.'

'There's something in that.'

'So that gives us plenty of time. Dave, what d'you say to steak and kidney?'

I watched him uneasily. George is always tricky to handle; facetious, he's impossible.

'Dave?'

'Oh sure. Anything you say.'

So we sat and ate whilst Williamson drank, and George conned him into promising to drive us to the Station and bring us back. He struck a hard bargain—we had to split the apple pie with him, and in the end the laugh was on us because it turned out to be just round the corner.

Thwaites wanted to see us both. As he put it, the firm. He had a nice tidy desk, nothing cluttering the place. It was all in his mind. No need for paper work, when you can do that. Now, without his hat, he looked older than I had thought, and more weary. He exercised his memory, and spoke.

'Mr . . . er . . . Martin and Mr. Cole.'

'Mallin,' I said, 'and Coe.'

George amplified. 'We thought it sounded better like that. I mean to say . . . Coe and Mallin! There's no magic in it.'

Thwaites plucked at his lower lip. 'There're things I'm not happy about,' he admitted. 'Your conduct in this business—your continuing interference in police activities.'

George looked at me. 'What's he on about?'

'The way you lost that BMW,' I suggested.

'Not,' said Thwaites sharply, 'that at all. I can't say I'm keen to hear you'd guard such a man. But he paid for what he got.' A tiny smile hovered, then dipped. 'And I'm quite disgusted at the very idea of expecting—of his expecting, but also of your going along with it—that you'd be able to establish something or other by some . . .' His voice tailed off. He'd lost himself in the sentence. He dragged his hands over his haggard face. 'You know what I mean.'

'Have you found the gun?' George asked.

'What? We're not discussing that.'

'Not discussing anything. Super, you *are* making a balls of this. We're miles ahead of you.' Aggressive, that was George.

'We do seem to be discussing something, after all,' the Super murmured patiently. He blinked. 'Just what I wanted to say. You made statements, both of you, but it now seems they were not full. If they had been, I could have got on to that MGB before you did. But no, there was no mention of that.'

'Oh, come on!' George appealed.

'Except in passing.'

'We were answering questions,' I pointed out.

'You're both ex-policemen. You'd know what would be useful to me. But you offered nothing.'

'Our duty to the client . . .' I gave it a try.

'Your client's dead.'

110

'So we owe him something.'

'You offered me nothing. You traced the MGB, and from that the driver of it. Then . . . no, listen to me, I've given you enough rope . . . then you went round there yourselves, before I could possibly have had the opportunity, and primed my best suspect to such good effect that she's got it off pat.'

I tried to look innocent. 'We were convinced of her innocence.'

'Of course you were. You persuaded her and she you.'

I was hurt; his contempt was so underplayed.

'She now believes implicitly in her own innocence,' he went on. 'She blinded me with her sincerity. But fortunately I've been insulated by a wife and two grown daughters. Miss Greaves's sincerity almost persuaded me to bring her in, but I decided that the sins of the daughters should not be visited on the suspects.' He whisked out a flashing white handkerchief and dabbed at his lips. Above it, his eyes were bright. 'Besides, there was the question of the gun. Seeing that you brought it up.'

Clearly there was something that I had not considered. George was sitting there, next to me, nodding, smiling.

'So you thought of that,' he said in admiration.

'I thought of it. But only after wading

111

through dozens of statements, and only because I was *looking* for a gun. A shotgun, Mr. Coe. And I found it. On paper, I must admit, but nevertheless there it was. Now let me see.' He steepled his fingers, dredging his memory. 'He said: "The big one came along and started throwing his weight about, and I tried to send him packing with my shotgun." You see—a shotgun. And he went on: "But the big oaf was too quick for me." '

'No,' said George, 'it didn't take speed. Fletcher was scared of it.'

'You took the gun from him.'

'Seems like I did him a good turn.'

'Perhaps you did. Let me make up my own mind about that. Tell me what you did with it afterwards.'

I could have kicked myself. I'd never given a second thought to Fletcher's shotgun.

George shrugged. 'I tossed it out of the car and into the ditch.'

'But where? That's what I want to know.'

'About half a mile down the road.'

'But out of sight of Fletcher?'

'Out of his sight.'

'You could show me on the map?'

'I could show you.'

I watched them, their backs to me, pouring over a wall map. 'There?' ' No, a bit further along.' Thwaites seemed tiny beside George, and was being very, very polite. What worried me was that George, too, was considerate, and deadly serious.

'You simply tossed it from your car window, driving past?'

'Just that.'

'You didn't unload it?'

'I was driving at the time.'

'Quite so. Well, gentlemen, it's been a pleasant chat.' It had not. We moved to the door. 'We must repeat it some time.'

I hoped not. There had been something deceptively deadly about Supt. Thwaites. I had felt that he'd been completely in control of the situation the whole time. George was silent as we left the Station, then seemed to hesitate, uncertain what to do next.

'Did you tell him the truth, George?'

'What's the matter with you, Dave?'

'I'm not happy. Shall we go on using the Renault?'

'Where to now? Some other wild goose chase?'

'To that point you had your fat finger on when you were studying the map. Do you want to use the Renault, I said.'

'I suppose so, if we're staying together.'

'Don't you think we should? They might not find the gun there.'

He glanced at me. 'I could be a few yards out.'

'You could be a mile out, with everything you say.'

He stopped dead. I turned and faced him

113

calmly, but it was an effort. He'd got his shoulders high, his fists huge in the pockets of that black monstrosity of a coat.

'We'd better get this straight,' he growled.

'So we should. You're acting strange, George.'

'Strange! The whole damned thing's been strange. I never thought I'd see the time when I'd act as guard for a rapist and murderer. I tell you, I've just about had a bellyful of it, and for just one snap of the fingers I'd pack it in and go home.'

I grinned up at him and snapped my fingers under his nose.

His right fist emerged and dashed my hand away. 'Right!' he shouted. 'That's it!'

Normally he would have laughed with me. He turned and stalked into the rear yard of the Crown and headed for the Renault. I caught him up and grabbed at his arm. He looked at my fingers.

'Take your hand off me, Dave.'

'Stop acting like a spoiled child.'

'I'm off, mate. Had it.'

'You can't just drive away. Your packing . . . What about . . .'

'You can do that. It's about your mark. Make the beds while you're at it. And pay the bill—I'll give you my half later. I can be fair, too, you know. Fair! I've had enough of your fairness. Lean over backwards, you do, seeing round things and through 'em, never straight

114

at 'em. I don't *care* who killed that bastard Collis. I wish him well, that's all.'

'All right, George, you go. When they get him—and they will, you know—I'll pass on your good wishes. Not that they'll do him any good. Me, I'm hanging around. Maybe I'll help to see they get the right one. Maybe I'll see round and through things enough to help him a bit with his defence. Who knows. But we owe Collis that much. If he was what you say, then we owe it to Collis to see that his murderer should get off as lightly as possible. George? Eh, George?'

'You're doing it again!' he shouted.

'I'm sorry.'

'Talk, talk. You blind anybody. Some day, Dave, I'm going to shut that mouth of yours.'

'But not today.'

'Oh . . . come on. You can bet those coppers'll never even find the place.'

Emotion ruins driving ability. George is a little hairy at the best of times, but now, his arms tense with the anger that hadn't really drained away, he took corners as an afterthought, and seemed to have forgotten where Monsieur Renault had put the footbrake

The frost had gone and there had been no more snow. Only in the deepest corners of the hedgerows was it still lying. The gutters ran deep. The squad of policemen were wearing waders in the ditch.

George parked the car a bit short. He got

115

out and scowled and watched them, as Thwaites strolled up. He must have moved fast, but police drivers can really cut through traffic when they wish.

'About here?'

'I was moving a bit fast.'

'From that direction?'

George nodded. 'Fletcher's got the end one of four terraced houses.'

'I know where Fletcher lives. Fast, you say. Running scared, they call it.'

'Shall we just say I was angry?' But calm now, coldly polite.

'There was nothing said about anger. Why were you angry?'

'Does it matter?'

'It could do.'

'That bullying pig! And he was proud of it. Have you spoken to Jonas Fletcher?'

'I have his statement. Also, of course, I had considerable dealings with him when his child died.'

'Tina,' I said. 'His step-child.'

'They seemed very close. Yes, I know Jonas Fletcher.'

'And did you ask him,' George demanded, 'why his precious Tina would be out at that time? This is country. No buses around here. No cafés. There'd be nowhere for her to go.'

'He'd taken the strap to her,' said Thwaites. 'His own phrase.'

George stared beyond him and said nothing.

116

'But she'd have been back,' I said. They looked at me. 'Fletcher said that. It seemed to matter.'

There was a short silence. Then George said: 'It's the wrong ditch.'

'What?'

'They're searching what was my near-side ditch. I threw it out of the driver's window . . . remember?'

'Then why did you stand and watch . . .'

'Just wondering how long it'd be before you realised.'

George had shaken Thwaites's control. He stalked away, and we heard him testily taking it out of the uniformed sergeant. It relaxed George. He turned to me, smiling.

'Nothing about that on the tape, Dave.'

'You mean about Fletcher? It didn't seem important.'

'Why did it matter to him that she would have been back?'

I laughed. 'George, George! Who was it said we shouldn't look round and through?'

'Can't I make an observation?'

'You're a fraud. A sentimental old fraud.'

'It was further this way, I'm sure.'

And he walked away, to take charge of the search calmly, to stand in the road and look round, and order them all a hundred yards along. A throwback to the old days; George wanted that gun. He'd been a weapon expert for the Midlands. The lure died hard.

Just before dusk they found it. A copper lifted his head with a cry of triumph, waving a double-barrelled 12-bore.

They clustered round. I remained with the car. Thwaites took it tenderly in his gloved hands, broke it open, snapped it shut again, then bore it off to his own car.

George walked back to the Renault. He seemed subdued; a reaction from the short-lived success. Police cars were streaming past us back to town.

He made no attempt to get in. 'It'd been fired. One barrel.'

'They'll be delighted. You said nothing of this, George.'

'How the devil would I know it'd been fired?'

'If it was fired at you, I meant, you'd know. People do. It's quite an experience.'

'You're not very funny. It was not fired at me.'

'You play things down, that's your trouble.'

'Did Fletcher say he'd fired it at me?'

'No. But he might, if we press him.'

'I tell you . . .'

'Don't you see how important this is? If it was not fired at that time, it's been fired since. Simple. And the only time since could have been into Collis's chest.'

'But I've just told you, Fletcher did not fire it at me.'

'I believe you, George. As things are, I'd be

118

excused for not doing so, but seeing that Fletcher can confirm it . . .'

He broke in dangerously. 'Are you going to question Fletcher to check on *me*?'

'I intend to ask him if it'd been fired before you went to see him.'

He thumped the car roof with his fist. 'You're going too far.'

'Let's go ask him.'

George angrily got into the driver's seat and stabbed at the throttle when the engine caught.

'And if it hadn't, big-head, what then?'

'Well then, I'm afraid we're going to have to wonder how Collis's murderer managed to find the gun, when a squad of coppers took nearly two hours.'

He glanced at me. 'It doesn't have to be the same gun. They've all got shotguns, around here.'

'That's so. But all the same, I'd like to ask.'

But we had spent too much time arguing, and Thwaites had beaten us to it. Or rather, Williamson had. Neither of us had spotted the one police car heading away from us. It was now standing outside the gate to the four terraces.

A local farmer, probably at the turn of the century from the look of them, had decided to build four farmworkers' cottages on a small knoll a hundred yards back from the road. Possibly he reckoned that they did not deserve protection from the elements. A farm gate opened onto a straight, churned driveway that led up the knoll. The cottages were nakedly exposed, no fences, no hedges, no gardens, just a bare expanse of battered earth forming enough of a yard to sling a clothes line across.

The squad car was parked down on the road. Williamson was just swinging the wide gate shut after him as he came out.

'The Super said you'd be along. He told me: Sergeant, be polite. Tell them what Fletcher says, the Super said. So I'm telling you. No, Fletcher did not fire the gun. Put two new cartridges in, and did not fire it. So there you are. No point in troubling him.'

'No point?' said George, watching the police car drive away. 'Of course there's a point.'

'You wouldn't get anywhere with that Fletcher character.'

George had his hand on the gate. 'Perhaps nobody's tried hard enough. He took a strap to his girl; perhaps somebody ought to do the same to him.'

'Now, George!'

There was a shout from up by the house. We looked up. The lights were on in the end one, none in the others. Perhaps they were empty. A figure, no more than a shadow, was running down the drive towards us.

'You get your bloody hand off my gate!'

George left it on. Jonas Fletcher came running up. He was panting; he would be, with

120

that chest.

'I've said all I'm goin' to, to the police,' he gasped. 'You take your dirty great fist off my gate.'

George glanced at me. 'Impetuous, ain't he?' He turned back to Fletcher. 'If I lift this fist from here, friend, there's only one place it's going.'

Fletcher took a step back. George grinned.

'I'm not answerin' any more questions.'

'Nobody's asking. You're not very important, Fletcher.'

'Questions, questions. Why can't they let my Tina lie in peace?'

'Tina?' said George, interested. 'Did the sergeant ask—'

'That Thwaites . . .'

'He's been here?'

'At the Station. You daft or somethin'? I reckon he must be. Got me there to ask about Collis, and where was I at the time . . .'

'And where was that?'

'Ask *him*,' Fletcher snarled. 'If you won't listen . . .' He looked sullen.

'We're not really interested, are we, Dave?'

'And besides,' I said, 'we don't believe a word of it. Why should he go on about Tina? That was a year ago. It doesn't make sense.'

'Well he did. He did!' Fletcher almost howled. 'Why'd he do that? You tell me. You two got the knowhow.'

And I could see that it really worried him.

121

'Do we owe him any favours, George?'

'I can't think of any.'

'I got a few cans of beer,' said Fletcher in invitation.

George laughed. He released his grip from the gate and reached over to pat Fletcher gently on the cheek. 'But how could we do that, friend Fletcher? We'd be your guests, in your own home, so how could we beat you up, in that event, and force you to tell us the truth?'

'There ain't any truth to tell.'

'Not from you.'

'That ain't what I meant. You got me all mixed up.'

'So what'd be the point, if you're all mixed up? Don't worry about it. Nobody's pushing you. We can get the truth from other people. Come on, Dave.'

'Heh . . .'

'Some other time, perhaps.'

Then stubbornly George marched back to the Renault, and though I hung behind for a moment, hungry for the chance that was slipping away, I knew that George would as soon as not drive away and leave me.

I slid in beside him.

'Why did you do that?'

'Scared him a bit. It doesn't do any harm.'

'We could've had a friendly chat with him. Who knows, with a few beers in him he might've relaxed enough. We might even have heard the truth of what happened that night when Tina died.'

'It's past history. What we've got to think about is Collis's murder.'

'That's occurred to you, has it?'

'And we can always go back again.'

'He might not be in the same mood, next time.'

'I meant when he's out. I reckon it'd be that road on the right.'

'Where to?' He was getting me confused.

'Firbelow.'

'Why when he's out?' I refused to be diverted.

'When he's in, he's not going to let us go upstairs. Dave, you *are* getting dim. Didn't you see that one bedroom window in the end wall? It faces towards the place where I threw the gun away, and it's way up high. I just thought— an idea, Dave, I do get 'em, you know—I thought I'd like to stand at that window, while you drove back there, and there's just a chance you can see it, over the trees.'

'You're crafty, George.'

'Ain't I?'

'If he'd seen where you threw it, then rescued it, and eventually used it on Collis . . .'

'What I thought.'

'Then, George, if he'd got any sense at all, and he's not stupid, he'd have cleaned it and replaced it with a new shell case in, back there in the ditch. And it'd have looked just the

123

same as when you threw it away.'

'Cold water, Dave. Who's tossing it now?'

'I just get the idea you're casting around, looking for confusing side-issues, and generally messing things up.'

'Just as long as you know whose side I'm on.'

'And why are we now going to see Delia Collis?'

'*She* knew Tina. I'm just wondering how. And if Collis did. Perhaps Delia can tell us why Tina went out that night.'

I looked sideways at him. The dashlights threw up at his face, and produced something wicked.

'She may not be prepared to discuss Tina's death. What we've got to concentrate on is her husband's.'

'Is it, Dave?'

'If you weren't driving I'd knock that smile off your face.'

'Smile? Was I smiling? It must be a trick of the light.'

CHAPTER NINE

The gate was open invitingly and there was no sign of Major. Life had returned to normal at Firbelow. Well . . . not quite normal, perhaps.

We were able to drive right up to the house,

and Delia had heard the car because she had the front door open as we climbed out. Major had his head thrusting forward under her armpit. He gave a welcoming woff when he saw George.

Delia seemed to be staring past us. It was now quite dark, so that there was nothing to see. But she frowned into the darkness.

'Did you notice anybody?'

George extricated himself from Major long enough to ask who she meant.

'It's why I brought Major inside,' she explained. 'There's no feeling of . . . of hatred, you understand. Nothing now, out there. But I got the impression there's somebody . . . I'm sure I've seen movement by the gate. But if I walk down, there's nothing.'

'So you left the gate open as a kind of invitation?' I asked. She seemed completely unconcerned, so she had no fear.

'It's almost as though he wants to speak, but he's too afraid. Or too shy.'

'You say he. Nowadays it's difficult to tell.'

'I saw a man's bicycle, by the trees opposite.'

I looked at George, but he seemed inclined to belittle it. 'If there's anything he wanted to say, he could phone.'

His tone was dismissive. She considered him with uncertainty. Up to that moment she had seemed quite normal, but George had jolted her back to the reality of murder.

'But do come in. I'll make some tea.'

125

'We only dropped by in passing,' I told her.

'All the same . . .' She made for the kitchen, and we obediently followed. 'I insist.' Her voice became sharp. 'We can talk in the kitchen, if that's what you want.'

'We'd love tea, wouldn't we George?'

He grunted. The kitchen was a modern, labour-saving triumph of ingenuity, which would probably take only a month or two to learn how to manage. The electric kettle, I thought, probably worked by radio or laser beam; there was no cord. Then I realised that the cupboard top on which it was standing was a cooker, and what I had taken to be a cooker was in fact an infra-red or ultrasonic or something like that device for spitting a whole hog.

Major sprawled on the patterned, polished floor. She conjured cups and saucers from a sliding hole in the wall.

'I'm so glad you came,' she said, flashing us a smile over her shoulder. 'It's been on my conscience. I suppose I *do* worry about things, but I've kind of got this obsession to clear everything away—debts and things—and start again from scratch.'

'A very good idea, too.' She would certainly have to start again, and live her own life. It was just a little soon, that was all, to become so practical.

'So I'll give you a cheque, and that'll be the end of it.'

'That wasn't why we came, Mrs. Collis.'

'Now, now. We don't have to be polite, do we! I mean, it's business. It's *your* business, and you've got to live.'

'There's no hurry at all. A statement . . . in the post . . .'

'I want to get clear of it.' Her head was down, but there was no need to read her expression. Her voice was breaking in her attempt to control it.

'There'll be expenses to calculate.'

Then she looked up. Her eyes were violent. 'Take a round figure. I don't care. Any figure.'

I laughed, pretending not to notice. 'We could cheat you . . .'

'If you didn't come for your money, then what for?'

'There're still things to clear up.'

'After he's dead?' she cried. '*That* was when it ended. I shan't pay you for a minute since then.'

'Of course not.' I was aware that George was ambling around the kitchen, and even more aware that he had remained silent, when I expected an interruption at any moment. 'I'm surprised,' I went on, 'that you'd be willing to pay us for our work even until then. After all, we failed.'

'I simply want an end to it.'

'Or at least, we failed in half of it. The other half we haven't yet completed.'

Her brow was flexed in concentration. 'I

127

don't understand.'

'Your husband expected us to prove his innocence.'

I tossed it in. From what Amanda had said, that expectation was now way in the past. I was simply wondering if it had any validity for Delia.

'The kettle's boiling,' said George equably.

She tore her mind away from what I had said, and went over to the kettle. I didn't see what she had to do to turn it off.

'Is that why you came?' she asked at last. Somehow her voice was normal again.

'In a way.'

'Only in a way?'

'If I were to ask you about Tina, it would be because her death might have some relevance to your husband's murder, and not necessarily to his innocence.'

She brought the pot to the table, frowning. 'You're trying to confuse me. Of *course* my husband's death is linked with Tina's. Or with one of the others.' How could she calmly pour tea, not spilling a drop, whilst she said such a thing? Or with one of the others! Her eyes were bright when she raised them. 'One of the three men must have managed to get to him.'

'Because they assumed he had killed the three girls?'

'Is there any doubt about that?' she asked sharply.

'Doubt about what?' I was gentle. 'That they

128

assumed it . . . none at all. That Adrian killed them . . .'

'Three sugars in mine,' said George, dead on cue, because I hadn't known how to finish the sentence. He saved me a shrug.

Amanda had given her own evidence of Adrian's guilt. Delia had no such direct evidence. All she could know would have to be from inference, from her knowledge of his inner character, and of his emotions. She slowly sat down at the table, and absently stirred her cup.

'Of course,' she said, staring at it, 'you were bound to ask. I could see it coming. You want to know how I knew, and why, and all I can say is that it was a feeling. Even now, there's nothing I can look back to and say: yes, I knew then, at that very moment. But he was . . . I suppose you'd call it secretive. There was something not quite genuine in his attitude to me. Some guilt he wouldn't tell me.'

The spoon stopped. She lifted it from the cup and tinged it against the side, casually, quietly.

'Why wouldn't he tell me!' she said with suppressed violence. There was a louder ting. 'Didn't he trust me? Did he think I'd go running to the police? But I was his *wife*. I owed him loyalty. To me, Adrian was my life. We were a couple, not two people. He should have known he could rely on my loyalty.'

She clashed the spoon against the cup, her

suppressed emotions contained in that single gesture. I thought they should have got together some time, she and Adrian, he with his hidden loyalty, she with hers rampant. But something had held them apart, something perhaps too cold and practical and passionless in Delia?

'Your loyalty must have been obvious,' I assured her. 'He must have known he could confide in you with safety.'

'But he did not do it!' she cried. Crash, the spoon went, and the cup shook with it.

'Then doesn't that suggest there wasn't anything to confide?'

'He didn't trust me,' It was like an incantation, accompanied by clashing bells. 'What did I care what he did!'

'Within reason, surely. You couldn't condone—'

'He cheated me!' she burst out, and the cup shattered, bursting tea all over the Formica, pooling across the surface to drip, then pour onto her lap, as she sat, suddenly, in desperate tears, his deception at last recognised.

We did not move. It was nothing we could interfere in, her strange grief. Her mute loyalty had been thrown back in her face, because Adrian had cheated her by failing to confide in her. She had longed for him to go to her and say he was a rapist and a murderer, and then she could tell him it didn't matter.

I said quietly to George: 'We'd better leave.'

'I'll wait a bit.'

The little woman complex? He was looking at her with the same hurt and puzzled concern as Major, who had come to his feet, startled, and was watching her with his head on one side.

'How do you think you can help, George?'

'I just want to know something. How can she say she didn't care what he did, when she knew at least one of the girls—Tina?' It was beyond poor old George's conceptions. He'd have raged with compassion.

She had obviously heard what George had said, but she ignored it. She got up suddenly and whipped open a drawer, withdrew a small kitchen towel, and began mopping up the mess. It was an automatic action; her eyes were glazed. Then:

'Excuse me.'

Or maybe I read it in her face. Anyway, she walked out, and we waited self-consciously until she returned in five minutes.

Women can walk through a tunnel lined with familiar and comforting adjuncts to their very existences, and from them draw strength. The tunnel itself might become depleted, but that is not what is seen; it is their private tunnel. She returned in a dark skirt, her face replenished and yet unmasked, her eyes calm.

'So very silly of me,' she apologised. 'You mentioned Tina. A dear child, but painfully . . . I was going to say shy, but more constrained, I suppose. She used to come here and help me with the cleaning, when we first built the place.'

'Did she speak of her mother?' I asked, thinking that perhaps Tina had been looking for a substitute.

'She didn't mention her. She spoke of her step-father, Jonas . . . Fletcher, isn't it?'

'Surely you knew her name.'

'She called herself Tina Martin. She refused to change it to his. She could please herself, I suppose.'

'Refused?'

'She hated him.'

'It's not what we heard. I thought they were very close. That's how Fletcher put it.'

She seemed to wince, then grimaced. 'I suppose he would.' She was silent.

'Would you care to explain that?'

'Not really.'

'Did your husband know her?' I went on, sliding onto a new tack.

'He met her here. If you mean, would she trust him, would she accept a lift in his car— yes, she would. I've had all this over with the police.'

'We're not preparing a case against him, you know.'

'Your attitude seems very strange to me, that's all.'

'I'm sorry about that. Every now and then I come up against a brick wall. Such as Tina and her stepfather.'

'You don't let anything pass, do you! I suggest you ask somebody else, then, somebody more her own age.'

'You've got somebody in mind?'

'Young Andrew Partridge. Tina was a friend of his wife, Marilyn.'

'Then we must certainly speak to him.'

'Why?' she asked wearily. 'What is there to gain, now?'

'I don't know. The truth, perhaps.'

Major saw us to the door. Delia remained behind. I patted Major's nose, and nearly caught it in the door.

'And what did you get from that, Dave?'

I said: 'Shall I drive?' I was aching for the touch of a wheel—my personal tunnel, I suppose.

'Try her if you like.' He walked round to the other side. 'Where did it get you?'

'You too. You're interested in Tina, as much as I am.'

'I'm interested in having no more to do with this.'

'George, just give me one clue, will you, just one hint of what the hell you *are* interested in.'

'The ignition key's in.'

'I can see that.'

'Then why don't we go and ask Andy Partridge about Tina?'

I glanced at him

'It's what you want, Dave. I'm just going along for the ride.'

The ride was short. Andy's cottage was only four miles from Firbelow, towards the town for a few hundred yards, and then off to the right. He was just putting away his motorbike in the shed he had.

He ignored us, although he must have been aware that we were standing just outside. It was a neat little shed, with a small bench and shelves up there in the shadows above the single, swinging shade. He took off his crash hat and carefully put it in the box-like container he had on the back of the bike, removed his black, zipped jacket—real leather, I thought—and unzipped his fleece-lined boots. Then at last, in slacks and sandals, he deigned to notice us.

'You got a pushbike in here?' George asked.

'Does it look like it?'

'Mrs. Collis has seen a man hanging round her place with a pushbike.'

'Not me, mate. I'd go on this.'

'Of course you would. Just asking.'

'If that's the lot, I'll get in for my tea.'

'Back to work, then?'

'I was feeling better.' He looked at us in disgust. 'I *was*.'

'A friendly chat,' I said persuasively. 'A friendly visit. We wanted to talk about Tina.'

He looked us up and down. 'Everybody does. What'd I know that could interest you?'

This was a new and more aggressive Andy.

134

Suddenly mature, a man of the world, who'd seen it all and didn't like it.

'She was a friend of your wife—Marilyn, isn't it?'

'They were friends.'

I was trying to soften him. 'Went to school together, I suppose.'

He sighed. 'Tina was just a kid. My wife was five years older.'

'But they were friends?'

'Fletcher's place is only half a mile down the road. Where's this getting? I want my tea.'

'Tina came here, to the cottage? It seems reasonable.'

'She came here. Yes.'

'And the girls would talk—they do, you know, all sorts of personal rubbish, embarrassing to chaps like us.'

'I used to go out.'

'But you'd hear things.'

'I tried not to listen.'

'But why not? You should've seen your face then. What was it you just remembered? It must have been unpleasant.'

'Nothing.'

'Fletcher's unpleasant,' I reminded him.

'I don't have anything to do with him.'

'But Tina did. More than she'd wish, I'd expect. Did she speak of that?'

The light was still swinging, impelled by some draught or other, lifting a shadow up and down the side of his face The corners of his eyes caught the reflection. It made him look wild.

'She spoke of it.'

'So that on the night she died, if she ran out of the house, she might conceivably come here?'

'Not here!'

'Now you sound violent.'

'I couldn't have her here. He'd fetch her back. That Fletcher's a crazy man. There's no knowing what he'd do.'

'But you've already said she often visited. Why should he fetch her back?'

'If she came to stay, you fool.'

'Ah!' I felt we had reached a turning point, but I could not see it. George said: 'If she couldn't come here, where would she go?'

'I don't know. Don't ask me. There's an aunt at Kings Bromley.'

'A fair way to walk,' George said. 'All of twenty miles. Well, well.'

I turned to him. 'Well, well—what?'

'Nothing.'

We both turned. A car had drawn up behind the Renault. The headlights went out and two shadows advanced through the gate. Sgt. Williamson seemed almost apologetic.

'We'd like you to come along with us, Mr. Partridge. The Super wants to ask you a few questions.'

'Heh, now look! I only just got home.'

Then I noticed that a van had drawn up

quietly behind the patrol car. It was more than questions.

'Are you arresting him?' I asked.

'I'm not sure what the Super's got in mind.'

'But you know the evidence he might be holding.'

'It'll take time, Mr. Mallin. Time. We'll need your bike, Mr. Partridge. Don't worry, it'll be quite safe in the van. And your boots, sir, and your riding jacket. Are these them? Fine. We'll feed you at the Station, and with a bit of luck you might be in your own bed again tonight.'

'A bit of luck?' I asked. 'What've you got, Sergeant?'

'A footprint or two, up at the log house. A tyre print of a motor cycle. And, if things go right, a confession. Then you'll be able to go home.'

We watched them drive away. That minor road might have been in the middle of nowhere, the activity there was in that area. When the car engines had died, there was silence apart from the slight breeze in the trees and the gentle whoosh, whoosh as the shade swung backwards and forwards.

'Williamson missed it,' said George with satisfaction. He pointed.

The shadow chased up and down the wall. At its highest pitch it revealed two inches of the shelf along one side.

'Well, will you look at that!' I said.

Andy Partridge had three different crash helmets on that shelf, two full-face ones like space helmets, and one visored one with a peak. One was red, one yellow, and one black.

'And the one he was using tonight was blue,' I remembered.

'And look at this.' George reached it down.

It was a black, crumpled shape in leather, with a long zip.

'What is it?'

'Haven't seen one of these in years.' George was going all nostalgic. 'I ran a Vincent Black Prince once. Now *there* was a bike! A thousand twin, a V, used to go bubble-bubble, all out of phase, until you opened it up. They were famed for the finish of the black and gold tanks. It was so splendid you were scared of scratching it. So a firm brought out a leather cover for the tank, only it was such a beautiful bit of leather you were scared of getting petrol or oil on it, so some other firm brought out a plastic cover for that.'

'Get to the point, George.'

'This is a leather tank cover.'

'You could've said so.'

'I was reminiscing. You've got no soul, Dave.'

'What I've got is a nasty feeling. A motorcyclist, on the road he's much like any other. In the rear-vision mirror he is, anyway. The only thing you can tell 'em by, at a glance, is the crash hat and the tank colour. So . . . if you ring the changes . . . How many crash hats can you get in those boxes they've got?'

'Sure to be two, Dave.' George got his reminiscing look again. 'No point in having a dual seat unless you've got a bird on the back.'

'And I suppose this Vincent of yours had a dual seat?'

'It certainly had. But they had a most unusual swinging fork arrangement—'

'Another time, George. What've we got? We've got a motorcyclist who could change his appearance in a second or two. And what better tailing vehicle is there than a bike? It can drop right back, knowing it can cut through the traffic again. This Andy chap has been tailing us.'

'Tailing somebody, anyway.'

'Listen. You know him. He's quiet, the determined type. He wasn't sure, he said, about Collis. He'd have to be sure. And then he'd kill him.'

'He's not the type. Not in cold blood.'

'Isn't he? It's the quiet ones who stick at it, all obsessive, and the quiet ones who do it in the end. But . . . and this is the point . . . if he wanted to be sure, and if he thought on the same lines as Collis, then he'd think that Collis's coming out of prison would mean another rape and another murder. So he *would* follow Collis, and conveniently he went on the sick list when Collis came back on the scene.'

'You do manage to make things sound real,

Dave. But there's no proof.'

'They've got a footprint and a tyre print.'

'Most motorcycle tyres are alike.'

'You're doing it again. Can't bear to find out who killed him, can you?'

'Dave,' he said kindly, 'don't get so excited. At the best it shows he could've been following. It doesn't make him a murderer.'

'But you said yourself you had the feeling of being followed.'

'As I would do,' he said irritably, 'if I was watching Collis, and Partridge was following him at the same time.'

'And what if he switched? What then? You see what I'm getting at? He could've been around when you took the gun from Fletcher. Damn it, that's only half a mile down the road. And admit it, a motorbike around—you wouldn't particularly notice it.'

'I tell you, there was not a soul around when I chucked it into the ditch.'

'Sure?'

'Of course I'm bloody sure.'

Our eyes met. An idea had begun to course through my mind. Perhaps it showed.

'I wish you hadn't said that, George. Not so definitely.'

'Want me to change my mind? D'you want me to tell lies, just to suit you?'

'Not to suit *me*.'

'Damn you, Dave.'

He marched back to the car.

CHAPTER TEN

It was unlike George to react so slowly. He had driven a good hundred yards before he drew in, his rear wheels on the grass verge.

'What the devil did you mean by that?'

'Use your brains. You toss a gun into a ditch, a fully-loaded gun, if we're to believe Fletcher . . .'

'No reason for him to lie about that,' George growled, hunched round in his seat.

'And when it's found it'd been fired. Now you have to be so damned awkward as to insist that nobody could've seen you dump it.'

'You're being too clever.'

'Logical.'

'You could've asked me. Instead of arguing all the time, you might just have said: George, isn't there a logical explanation?'

'And what would George have said?'

'He'd have told you that a gun can go off if you throw it around. A finely-trimmed trigger, a branch, anything like that.'

'But nevertheless you'd still like to look at the view from Fletcher's end window?'

'Wouldn't you?'

It was all friendly enough, a reasonable discussion between partners. But George knew what I had suspected, and the resentment was there in his voice, veiled, but there.

141

'So all right,' I said. You can't apologise to George.

And as he tried to pull out, a cyclist without lights swerved violently to avoid the off-side wing, and for a moment was held, wobbling and frantic, in the dipped heads.

'That's Goldwater,' I said, and he had come from the direction of Firbelow.

George juggled with the clutch, and the tyres spun on the soggy grass. He cursed, wrenching the wheel, and the car bucked, tilted its nose upwards, then plunged forward. George righted it.

'Stable old bitch!' he shouted. 'I'm getting to like her.'

We set off in pursuit.

A length of downhill had assisted Reuben Goldwater. He must have been doing a very precarious thirty when we came up behind him. I'm sure George only wanted a word, a quiet word, about hanging round the bungalow, and why, but he had to go and toot that horn, and as everybody knows there's a special effeminate aggresiveness about French warning devices. It probably scared the poor devil to death.

He wobbled, skidded, then dived into the ditch, right opposite Jonas Fletcher's gate.

George backed up until the headlights shone full on the scene. We jumped out and ran to his rescue. He was under the bike. I took the crossbar and George an arm, and together we hauled them out, wet and bedraggled, but as far as we could see, still serviceable.

Goldwater was jabbering, incoherent with indignation. '. . . the hell you're playing at . . .'

George heaved him up. 'Only wanted a word, Mr. Goldwater. We didn't mean to startle you.'

Goldwater had at last recognised him. His jaw became locked between 'stupid' and whatever word might have best linked with it, and, while he was staring, an avalanche descended on us and scattered all three of us into the ditch.

George came up fighting. I got off my knees quickly enough to restrain him, or Jonas Fletcher would have been nursing a broken jaw.

Fletcher stood above us. 'You leave him alone! I saw that. Assault! I'll 'ave the police on ya.'

George straightened slowly. Deliberately he ran his fingers down the whole muddied length of his coat. 'I wanted a word,' he whispered. 'Quietly and without fuss. Now you . . .' He jabbed Fletcher in the chest with a forefinger like a marlin spike. '. . . you, friend Fletcher, just get away from me. Now, Fletcher. Away!'

'Please do it,' I said, not wishing to see blood.

Fletcher backed away. George paced around the front of the car. I went to the

143

passenger's door. George said: 'Don't hit him, Dave. I want him alive.' I got in the car, and George drove away.

I suffered. One elbow had contacted a pedal. I was in agony, otherwise I would have asked to drive. I should have insisted. For one panic moment a deer stood stark in the lights, then sprang away. George slowed to sixty. The car steadied. His voice was even.

'We could've belted him then, Dave, carried him into the house, then while you phoned the doctor I could've got up to that room.'

'You didn't think, that's your trouble. You're getting slow.'

He grunted. His damp coat smelt of stale glue.

When we got a look at the damage, it wasn't too bad. The black coat would need a dry cleaner and my elbow a plaster. George was more relaxed. A touch of violence does him the world of good.

'Coming down for a drink?'

'It's barely opening time,' I said.

'We're guests!'

'I'll see you in the bar, then.'

I went out into the street. It was unreasonably mild for February, and the mists were creeping in already. Down there in the valley it came in from all sides, with no way out. The streetlights were dismal, and footsteps echoed. From a café opposite, hard rock pounded out, stirring the mist, and a

144

woman screamed. It was nothing: they're always screaming. A motorcycle revved away with open exhausts.

In the entrance hall to their chic new Station, I asked for Sgt. Williamson. The desk sergeant was doubtful about it but said he would try, and what was that name again?

Williamson ambled down a corridor after about five minutes, during which I read the poster about the man wanted for rape and murder. They hadn't taken it down. Didn't they think they'd caught him?

'Just enquiring,' I said.

'No harm in that.'

'You charging Andy Partridge?'

'Well now . . . there's harm in that. You surely don't expect a reply.'

'A hint. You've got a footprint or two . . .'

'They fit. But d'you know, Mallin, they all wear loose boots. Something to do with warmth. Size 10 is the most popular. Now isn't that a bit of bad luck!'

'And the tyre tread?'

'Fits. But there again, a nearly standard tyre for that sort of bike. Three two five by sixteen. Would you believe that?'

'From you, Sergeant, yes. And the jacket?'

'We were lucky there. Sort of. It's real leather. Plastic and he could have washed it clean. But not leather. We reckoned, you see, that with a close shot, there'd be some spray of blood. Spots and speckles on the chest, that's

145

what we looked for.'

'And you found them?' I couldn't understand his attitude.

He shook his head, pursing his lips. 'On the chest, no. But there's the damndest thing, there was blood on the back.'

'So you reckon he fired over his shoulder?'

'It's a mistake to confide in you, I can see that.'

'And the gun?'

'The one we found? Ah . . . now, here's a thing about shotguns. You can't pin them down to one specific gun. No rifling, you see.'

I nodded solemnly, humouring him. 'You're not sure it's the one you found?'

'It's just one of a thousand shotguns around here.'

'But it had been fired.'

'One barrel. The ballistics people say it could've done that itself. Impact. There's such a thing as a hair trigger, Mallin.'

'I'd heard.'

'And there's such a thing as medical evidence that the wound wasn't made with just one barrel. Collis got the charge from two. Isn't that convenient?'

'Not for Thwaites. And I bet Partridge has never owned a shotgun.' He nodded. His eyes were watching me carefully. There was no sign of disappointment in his expression; he was simply keen and intense. 'So,' I went on, 'you'll hardly be able to hold him.'

'I wouldn't say that. We like to put on a show.'

'You're cynical. The poor young bugger must be suffering.'

He laughed flatly. 'Can you hear the screams? If you do, it'll be Thwaites. It's a tough one, this.'

He was too bland. Too co-operative. The eyes never left me, measuring my reactions. I tried to be casual.

'Don't push it too far. You'll make a martyr of him.'

He grinned as I turned away. I looked back after two paces. He hadn't moved; his eyes hadn't moved.

'Tell your big friend,' he said, lifting his chin.

'About what?'

'The gun and the trigger.'

'He's figured it out for himself.'

I left, tense, feeling that he was tempting me to continue with it. Perhaps he had expected me to argue about it being a two-barrel discharge. I wouldn't dare. George is the expert. George would argue it, because, even to my relatively inexperienced eyes, that had looked like a single-barrel discharge.

I reached the Crown before I saw that this was what he wanted. I stopped and lit a cigarette. My motoring coat was inside, with drying mud flaking from it. It was colder than I had thought, but I could not yet face George. I started a circuit of the town square, which was guarded by a pedestrian rail.

The metal was damp to my right hand. I felt like an old man, reaching for it, but for a moment I had wanted security. There are things in life you rely on because they are always so, always there as you expect. But sometimes you reach for support and abruptly the security is no longer there. A wall, or a convention, or a myth crumbles away.

I moved away from the rail. My hand had slipped on it, and I resented its false offer, even as I hated my sudden desire for solid reality. The square was not the place to be in, in that frame of mind. Nothing was real. Depth dissolved into grey, and across the open space there was nothing. I realised I was walking faster, and deliberately slowed. Let my mind race, but my legs deliberate! I crossed one street before I noticed it was policed by traffic lights. I searched for the next, and cursed my agitation when I went on and on, and seemed to have lost it. The traffic had melted away. I reached the lights, abruptly and weirdly above my head, and deliberately stepped out, inviting the comforting hoot of a horn. But no car crossed my path.

Ahead of me, light streamed in strained white across the pavement from the café. I felt the impact of the amplifiers. Again the woman screamed, and I realised it was what they called singing. The café was empty, the sound itself a ghost. Perhaps it was a man's voice after all. Unreality pursued me, but the sound seemed to cling to me.

I was nearly running when I reached the Crown again. The light from the public bar was warm. I was utterly chilled. I turned into the car park, rejecting the comfort.

George had left the Renault unlocked. I slid in and sat behind the wheel. He always left his vehicles unlocked, as a challenge to life. Touch my car if you dare! I had to quell an overwhelming desire to start it up and drive straight out to Filsby, and have a look at that phone box. Ridiculous. And in any event, why not use the Porsche? It would be feeling neglected.

But the tenuous warmth of the Renault held me. I lit another cigarette and wished I'd got my pipe, and searched around for the tape recorder we had been using. Senseless to drive out to Filsby. Of course the number in that box was as George had said, otherwise he would not have invited me inside it to phone Collis's office. He'd have known Dave Mallin's well-known reputation for remembering such details as the number of the box he's phoning from. The trouble was that Dave Mallin couldn't remember it, and it didn't help to fight it. You had to relax—which was out of the question.

I played with the recorder's switches. You drop in at all sorts of places. My own voice:

'*. . . going to go insane, sitting in this damned car park. Why doesn't he do his trips when I'm on, that's what I want to know. You get all the fun, George . . .*'

That was before Collis took me up to the log house. Before George's trips were all of a sudden not so much fun.

I wound on a few feet and pressed the Play again.

'*. . . was going to mention that, Dave . . .*'

Mention what? I re-wound and tried again. My voice:

'*. . . I was thinking we ought to lay on some system in case of emergency. Phone back to the pub, George, how's that, and always be on hand . . .*'

Funny, I didn't remember saying that, but I'd been on hand when it happened. There's a special thing about phones. You never know where your caller is. He could say he's in the next street, and he could be in Scotland. He could say he's calling from Filsby 73, and be miles away at the time. Close enough to get to Filsby 73 before I could, but not actually there.

Lay off, Dave. Get inside and ask George about the double-barrel discharge. Go on, man, this is doing you no good.

I flipped the wind button, searching for it. And got it.

'*. . . slipping out under my nose, the crafty so-and-so. No, there she is. What's all the dawdling for?*'

150

I wound on a bit.

'. . . *pulling out a few stops now. Wish I'd got the Porsche. Come on, you beauty. That's my girl . . .*'

I flipped again.

'. . . *look at that, will you! Two bloody great trailers. I ain't going through that till she's clear . . .*'

I cut it, wound back, and tried again.

'. . . *ain't going through that till she's clear. Easy now. That should do it. Cor strike—the spray! Clear through, now. Where you gone, you bitch! Where you gone?*'

I sat with the machine silent on my lap. I wanted to run through more, but I couldn't face it. Silently to myself, comfortingly, I repeated his own words to me. 'Stable old bitch. I'm getting to like her.' All cars are female to George; he has a sentimental attachment to them; they respond to him. George, did you mean the car? Did you, George? Or the driver?

Ridiculously, almost self-consciously and certainly ashamed, I put on the interior lights and searched the back seat, where he might have tossed Fletcher's shotgun, and where it might have left no trace apart from a smear of gun oil. I don't know whether I was pleased to detect nothing. It could have lain there, or on the carpet behind the front seats, for days, and left no sign. Until the time came to use it, and *then* toss it into the ditch.

But *that* gun had been fired only once.

151

Miserably I forced myself to climb from the car. I locked it, not having George's faith in humanity, and took him the keys.

He was in the public bar. George is a man who likes company, and delights simply in watching movement, and listening to human noise. The bar was filling. George was at a table with a pint of bitter and a huge pile of sandwiches. His face was warm, his eyes amused.

'Enjoying yourself?' I asked.

'Where's your drink?'

'He's bringing it. What's so funny?'

'Those two over there. Fletcher and Goldwater. Every minute or two Goldwater tries to get up from the table, and Fletcher drags him back.'

'Perhaps Fletcher's treating. His birthday.'

'No. Goldwater's trying to get to me.'

'He's fallen for your charms.'

He grinned. 'He's terrified, Dave.'

I put the keys under his nose, and my beer arrived. I said I'd share George's sandwiches and he said you won't you know, so I ordered cheese and told George he'd left his car unlocked.

'Nobody's ever pinched one of mine.' His voice was even. 'Why'd you go to the car, Dave?'

'To listen to the tape.'

'They're at it again. Look.'

Sure enough, Goldwater was trying to get to

152

his feet, and his eyes were for us. Fletcher's hand was clamped on his arm.

George bit into a sandwich. 'Hear anything interesting?'

I find it difficult to lie to George. For one thing, because he sees through you, and for another, because I expect him to tell me the truth.

'Not a thing,' I lied, because I wasn't sure he had. 'I've spoken to Williamson, too.'

'Ferreting all the time. You're not going to get anything out of him.'

'He said the same thing as you, that the gun could have gone off on impact.'

'You see . . . they're not as daft as they seem.'

'But you didn't hear it go off?'

'Can't say I did. It'd be muffled, firing way down the bottom of a ditch, and I was accelerating hard.'

'Was somebody after you?'

He considered me, then shook his head. 'Dave, you know me. I'm impulsive. I have to control myself. There was this Fletcher, just tried to blow my head off . . .'

'You said he didn't fire it.'

'I was speaking figuratively. Good Lord, I've got to spell everything out for you. He'd pointed it at my head, Dave. I'm fussy about my head; I live in there. So I was mad. If I didn't get away quick, I'd have done something nasty and probably permanent to his face.'

153

'That sounds like you, George. Still, we don't have to go near him again.'

'How come?' He seemed unsuspicious still.

'Because that wound in Collis's chest was from the discharge of two barrels. The gun from the ditch had only one fired. So it doesn't signify what you might be able to see from Fletcher's window.'

He put down his glass. For a moment he leaned forward, staring down at it, then quickly his head came round and he was looking at me sideways.

'Is that the truth?'

'I don't know whether it's the truth. It's what Williamson said.'

'It was he doing the lying, then.'

'As a change from me?'

'You're saving me from saying it.'

I steered round it. 'You want it to be that gun, don't you, George?'

He did not answer at once, then: 'You know how we've always worked. You did it your way, and I did it mine, and somehow, when we got it together, something came out of it. But we had to get together. We had to trust each other, Dave.'

'You don't have to go on . . .'

'I know your methods. I know your twisted kind of chat, implying, sliding in bits, linking up unrelated remarks. You're using it on me. I can't say I like it.'

'I didn't think you'd realise.'

'So it's all right if I don't?'

I was wishing he wasn't so sad. Like a great, hurt sheepdog, he studied me, wondering what he'd done to deserve it. You can't look into eyes like that and not relent.

'I think you killed Collis, George.'

He raised his glass and paused, then he lifted it towards me, his eyes mocking. 'To you, Dave. At least, you've got round to being honest.' He took one great gulp. 'Mind you, not honest enough. If you really looked at yourself—try it, Dave, some time, one honest look—you'd admit that if you really thought I'd done it you'd be slapping me on the back.'

'No!'

He laughed. 'And while you've been talking, he's slipped away.'

'What the hell're you talking about?'

'Reuben Goldwater, slipped his guard. He's gone out of the side door.'

'Not coming to us, then.'

'I'm disappointed. Maybe he thinks I killed Collis, too, and he only wants to say how happy he is, and could he have my autograph.'

'It's not funny.'

'You're changing, Dave. You used to like a good laugh.'

'I don't understand you any more.'

'Then you see where that gets us? You lie to me, you don't trust me, you don't understand me, and you can't laugh at me. I could sell the Renault. She's still unmarked.'

155

'She, George?'

'Sell the car and plough the money back, and I'll go my own way. Elsa would understand.'

'Elsa would kill me if I let you go. She loves you, George.'

He laughed easily. 'That's more like it.'

'She'd kill me if I let you go to prison.'

'Let's go and see where they've gone.'

'For God's sake!'

'Fletcher went after him.'

We went to look. Goldwater's bike was in the side yard, leaning against the outside gents that wasn't used any more. Goldwater was using it now, though. He was sprawled inside, his face mashed, his body twisted in a nasty way, and barely managing those rasping, raking breaths a man takes when his ribs have been broken in and they're as near as damnit piercing his lungs.

CHAPTER ELEVEN

I was in front. 'Get to a phone, George.'

'Don't move him.'

'Of course not. Where's your coat?'

'Upstairs drying,' he said as he left.

I put my jacket under him. Goldwater was attempting to speak.

'It's all right. Lie still. Don't try to say

156

anything.'

He made a tremendous effort. I reached over and held his head.

'Trying . . . not to,' he croaked.

I didn't think I'd heard him correctly. 'Nothing you need to say, old chap. There's nobody here but me. Now just lie quiet. My mate's gone to get an ambulance.'

'Gone and come back,' said George, dropping on his knee beside me. 'How is he?'

'I wish to God he wouldn't keep trying to say something.'

Goldwater was fighting the pain, but every breath he took was agony, and he was continuously licking his lips.

'Not saying . . . anything,' he managed to get out.

'No need to,' I assured him.

The face twisted. He heaved, and managed to say:

'I'm not tellin' . . . you . . . a thing.'

'Of course you're not. We're not even listening. Are we, George?'

'I'm not, anyway.'

'My friend's not listening,' I said in a comforting tone.

'You do what . . . what you like, I ain't going to say . . .'

The eyes were vague, glazed, staring beyond me and seeing something I wasn't aware of. Blood from his nose dripped off his cheek.

'We know you're not. Now Mr. Goldwater

. . . Reuben . . . it's really much better if you just wait quietly.'

Much better for us, too. The sweat was soaking my shirt, crouching down there so intimately close to his suffering.

'You tell him then.'

'Sure I will.'

'Tell him . . . tell him I wouldn't say.'

'I'll do that. We'll both do that. Won't we, George?' I asked desperately.

'We'll both tell him,' George promised. 'We'll tell him you wouldn't say.'

'Promise.'

'We have promised.'

'Tell . . . him.' It was important to him. He reached towards me for absolute assurance. What could I say but:

'Tell who, Reuben? How can I tell him, if I don't know who?'

'Easy, Dave,' George whispered.

'Quiet!' I put my head closer. 'My friend's listening again, Reuben. You whisper to me. Who do I have to tell that you wouldn't say anything?'

It's difficult to whisper when your breathing control is restricted. It came out in a great gasp of pain.

'Jonas . . . Jo . . .'

He lay back. I thought for one moment that we had lost him. I put my ear close to his lips, but all I heard was a frightening gurgle.

'It's all right, Reuben,' I told him. 'All right

now. I've got it. It's clear. I don't have to tell Jonas Fletcher anything, but if I do speak to him . . . Reuben, you hear me, I'm saying that if I do speak to him, casual like, and if he asks, I'll say you wouldn't tell me. There, isn't that what you wanted!'

I was so close to him that I could feel his fear. There was panic in the movement of his eyes. His tongue made small clicking noises. I knew that the effort was killing him, and that I had to calm his efforts. There was perhaps one word left in him, if I could find it, if I could coax out the right one to set him at rest.

'But Reuben . . . Reuben, listen carefully to me. If I talk to him . . . if I talk to Jonas and I have to tell him that you said nothing . . . Please, Reuben, try to understand. If I say you would tell me nothing, I've got to know what it was you said nothing about. Otherwise it might slip out. I've got to know what it is I must *avoid* saying. Reuben . . . if I speak to Jonas, what is it you haven't told me that I musn't mention?'

His brain clawed for it. I couldn't think of any other way to put it, and help him get it down to one word.

He strained his neck. I put a hand on his forehead.

'Case . . .' he groaned. 'Case . . . es.'

'That's it,' I crooned. 'That's a good lad, then. Now you can go to sleep. I understand. Not ever, Reuben, never will I tell Jonas that you mentioned cases. I will say you refused to

159

say anything about them. I will. I promise.'

He sighed. George said: 'They're here.' I hadn't heard the ambulance. I straightened, standing aside, leaning against the foul wall. The cubicle was suddenly flooded with light and two ambulance men took over efficiently. George seized my arm, rather too roughly I thought, and drew me aside.

'Dave,' he said warmly, 'I must congratulate you. You can be as big a bastard as anybody when you try.'

'I got it out of him.'

'You must be proud.'

'I don't feel too good.'

I went and got a brandy at the bar. We both had a brandy. When I looked round, I saw that the room was empty.

'Outside,' George explained. 'They've got to see him carried inside the ambulance. It makes them feel good. Good that it ain't them.' He poured the rest of his brandy down his throat. 'So what did your hard-earned information mean, Dave?'

My jacket was probably being trampled into the floor of that noisome old gents. The brandy helped, but still I was chilled and empty, and I wasn't going to be wearing that jacket again. I was trying to remember what I'd done to feel so exhausted.

'I get awfully tired of you playing dumb, George. You know as well as I do that Reuben Goldwater has been hanging around Collis's place, trying to work up the nerve to tell Delia something. Tonight he tried to come across to tell us something, only Fletcher stopped him. And earlier on, when Goldwater fell in the ditch, why was Fletcher so mad, unless he thought we were getting some information out of him? But it wasn't going to be long, George. Before very long, Coldwater would've bust at the seams if he didn't tell somebody. So he's been persuaded to keep his mouth shut. The persuasion went a bit far, but it doesn't alter a thing. Goldwater was beaten up to persuade him not to tell anybody about the cases.'

There was a bustle of movement outside, and a burst of voices as the bar door swung open. From the back, out in the street, a voice shouted: 'They got Andy Partridge for it,' and already the assault on Goldwater was a thing of the past. The throng that surged into the bar was chattering excitedly about the arrest of Andy for Collis's murder.

The side door, behind me, opened. 'Excuse me, sir, is this your jacket?'

Ambulance men are wonderful. Like nurses, who're angels; gnarled, lumpy angels insulated with some sort of distress-proof coating, otherwise they'd surely go insane.

He said: 'Sorry about the . . .' and coughed apologetically. He put it on the bar.

'Goldwater?'

He grimaced. 'Getting him in now. I wouldn't like to say.'

161

I tried to extract the essentials of my life from the pockets without touching it. George hoped I wasn't going to put it on, and I assured him there was no chance of that.

There was a steady exodus from the bar. I watched them leave.

'He'll have gone off home,' George decided. When I stared, he added: 'Jonas Fletcher.'

'Gone to hide his head. There's no direct evidence,' I warned him.

'But we should go and talk to him. It's our bounden duty. And if it becomes necessary to encourage him . . .'

'No, George!'

'All right. We'll just ask him, gently, about cases.'

'I promised Reuben.'

'Now Dave, that was just . . .'

'I gave him a promise!'

'No need to get upset. You *are* getting touchy. Then I'll ask him. I didn't do any promising. I didn't even hear what you promised you wouldn't do when you didn't meet Fletcher.'

I could not respond to the twinkle in his eye. 'I'll go and get another suit on. George . . . can you do something with the jacket?'

'I can face emergencies,' he said with dignity.

I went up and washed my face and looked at my eyes in the mirror because I didn't seem to be focusing too well, and slipped into my

Westmoreland tweed and the motoring coat that by then seemed about dry. And then, because I remembered a yearning for it, I dug out my pipe and pouch, and went down to pick up George.

No matter what he said and however he objected, I was determined that we were going in the Porsche.

He was talking to Williamson at the bar. Apart from those two, it was empty.

'The word goes around,' said the sergeant sadly. 'It's all over town that we've charged Andy Partridge. I wonder how it could've leaked out.'

'Then he *has* been charged?'

'As a matter of fact, Mr. Mallin, no. But that's the news that's flying around. I've been out and about. Everywhere I've been, I've heard it. Rumour is a vicious thing.'

'And now it's our turn to be told?'

He raised his eyebrows at me. 'Your turn to be asked. I've already questioned your friend. Now . . . what do you know about the Goldwater business?'

'Nothing.'

'You found him.'

'We were searching for the gents.'

'You're staying here. You'd know where to go. That hole out there hasn't been used in years.'

'You know how it is . . . ex-coppers. It's instinct. You have to know all the outside stalls in town.'

'Very good,' he approved. He looked from one to the other of us. 'Don't I rate the truth? Or have I got to assume that you two got him in there and tried to get information out of him?'

'We're ex-coppers all right,' George agreed, grinning so close to his face that the sergeant recoiled. 'We'd know how—as I'm sure you do, friend—without breaking things, without even a mark.'

'I'm warning you, Coe! I've heard things about you from the Super. He says he knows you.'

'Dear old Arthur. I didn't think he'd remembered. I'd marked him down as an eternal constable. I wonder how he made it.'

'So we play it the hard way?' said Williamson.

'You play it how you damned well please,' said George. 'Me'n Dave are going out. And just so you don't imagine you can keep a tail on us, we're using his Porsche. Isn't that so, Dave?'

'What? Oh yes . . . sure.'

He watched us leave. Theoretically, he could have taken us in for questioning. But I thought he looked relieved. Perhaps he only wanted us out of the way for a while.

The Porsche started at a touch. I eased myself down into the seat, re-establishing the intimacy. George was miserable beside me, his head against the roof lining.

'Get moving, Dave. Don't give him time to get a car round.'

'He won't be doing that. Anyway, I could drop him. We'll go the wrong way out of town.'

'We don't want a tour of the countryside.'

'It'd be nice if Fletcher was home. So we'll give him time.'

'I don't know about that.'

I took it steadily the wrong way out of town, then gradually opened out as the streetlamps fell behind and the dark, comforting night closed round us. We drove clear of the mist in five minutes. Up there, we had a moon. I was feeling good, for the first time in days, with the wheel alive under my hands.

'Left here,' said George. 'Cut through Boreton Wood.'

George can visually memorise a map. The realisation jolted me from my complacency. George had said, from Filsby 73—if I was to accept that—that he was lost. George is never lost.

'Right at the fork ahead,' he said.

'I saw the sign.'

'And perhaps a bit slower.'

We came down towards Fletcher's place from the direction of Firbelow instead of from the town. Because of this, we saw the outline of the row of four terraces from the end occupied by Fletcher. There were no lights visible. I drew in where they had found the

165

shotgun.

Now, with the sky brittle white and the moon only a few degrees to one side of the building, we could see the awkward shape of Fletcher's chimney, silhouetted clearly.

'Isn't that good enough for you, George?'

'Not really. Drive on to his gate.'

I braked to a halt outside Fletcher's house. The gate was open. George got out and stretched himself. I think it's exhibitionism, myself.

'Better back her up and turn round, Dave.'

I got his point, and did so. Then we left the car and walked up to the harsh and unwelcoming block of buildings. The silence caught my breath.

As I had guessed, the other three houses in the block were unoccupied. Window sills crumbled at the touch, and any of the doors could have been leaned-in. Fletcher's was a little more secure, and was one paint coat ahead of the others, but not much more than paint was preventing his glass from falling out.

George put his hand against the front door. 'One decent shove . . .'

But there's a difference between breaking and entering and unlawful entry. I knew there was no restraining George in his present mood, and in fact I had no wish to, but I preferred a more delicate approach.

'Let's try the back.'

The rise of the knoll continued behind.

There had been a feeble attempt at cutting back the earth, but the small space that remained level behind the back door was no more than four feet wide. During periods of heavy rain the mud would soak down and lie against the door. Because of this it had been permanently sealed. George prodded light from his penlight. We could see the nail heads.

'The window?'

It was shut, but the catch had rusted away. George's penknife eased through the pulpy wood and persuaded it open with a creak.

'I could get in there and go through and unbolt the front door,' I said, being as he was just about to suggest it.

'There won't be any bolts, or he couldn't fasten it when he went out.'

'I didn't see any lock.'

We glanced at each other, then went back to the front and had another look. There was a hole you stuck your finger through, with a latch inside. The door opened. We walked in.

Technically, we had broken and we had entered. An interesting point—had we broken and entered?

George said not to worry about that now, and was this all the furniture he'd got, and suggested he should go up to that end bedroom and see what there was to be seen from its window.

By that time I was losing my enthusiasm for the gun in the ditch. Thwaites had said there had been two barrels fired at Collis, and though it might have been a try-on, George wasn't going to convince me that anybody could have used Fletcher's gun but himself. But he gave me strict instructions. Drive to where they'd found the gun, and flash the tail-lights. Then come back.

I did. Then I backed up, swung round, and returned to Fletcher's. An ambulance was just driving away.

When I got up to the house the front door was wide open.

'Oh come in,' said Fletcher sarcastically. 'Help yourself.'

George was standing with his shoulder against the mantel of one of those old iron ranges, and Fletcher was trying to light the gas under a kettle on his black cooker with only one serviceable hand, his left.

George met my eye and nodded slightly. I said: 'Had some trouble?'

'He's broken his hand,' George explained. 'You tell him, Fletcher. I'm too ashamed to repeat it.'

The plaster cast, for a broken hand, was extensive, right up to the elbow. Fletcher looked sullen, and did not talk directly to me.

'These two blokes . . . could've been three, they got Goldwater in the pub yard. Me—I give it a try, but they was big buggers. Busted me 'and on one of 'em, though.'

'And promptly disappeared?'

168

He flashed a look of hatred at me. 'I wasn't gonna hang around there, mate.'

'But Goldwater was hurt.'

'I was runnin' to a phone box.'

'He's like as not going to die.'

He looked beyond me. 'That so?'

'You can't hit a man when he's only got one arm, Dave,' said George fairly. 'Take a look up the stairs. On the right at the top.'

'Heh, you look here . . .'

But Fletcher wisely made no move towards me. The stairs creaked horribly. They opened directly from a corner of the room, and proceeded upwards through a narrow cleft in the ceiling. There was no landing apart from a three foot by two foot level surface, with a door each side. The one on the right was open.

The light switch was hanging loose from the wall, where the plaster had broken away. The light, when I got it, was poor, from a naked bulb. The ceiling was open joists, with plaster-board laid upon them inside the loft. There had been some attempt to brighten the walls with pop star posters, and the curtains were a bit of rescued chintz with a blue and white stripe. The bed looked thin and discouraging, its top cover a brown army blanket. There was one cupboard—a kind of chest of drawers—in the room, but no wardrobe. A length of rope across one corner could well have been used to hang clothes. There were none on it now.

On the cupboard surface was lying a

powerful pair of binoculars. Beside it on the floor were two suitcases, small, the soft cover type, one blue and one brown.

I did not look out of the window. The drawers down one side of the cupboard, and the shelves in the other half, were empty. I flung the suitcases on the bed, confident that they would not be locked, as the keys would have disappeared years before.

Both contained womens' clothes. Girls', rather, because these must have been Tina's. Yes, Tina's. A tattered old teddy bear was packed down the edge of one of them. I shut them quickly; I'll never be able to examine other people's intimate possessions without shame.

When I got downstairs again, George was explaining to Fletcher the disadvantage of having a broken hand, and outlining in what way it prevented the wearer of a plaster cast from evading questions.

'He was just saying,' George told me, 'that he's taking her things to a jumble sale.'

'Her teddy bear, too?' I asked. 'See anything, George?'

'I saw your lights flashing.'

I nodded at Fletcher, smiling, trying to pretend to myself that I didn't hate him.

'All it means,' I explained, 'is that you could have seen where George threw the shotgun. Why the binoculars?'

'Tina's. She liked to watch the birds.'

170

'They'd be worth around twice as much as all the rest she owned. They're yours, Fletcher.'

'Please yourself. I like to watch birds, too.'

'He's being awkward,' said George, easing himself from the mantel.

'Let me ask him, George. Now, Mr. Fletcher, politely I'm asking you about those cases—upstairs.'

'Should you mention them, Dave?' George asked wickedly.

Fletcher glanced at him, frowning. 'I packed 'er stuff up.'

'I happen to know she'd spoken to other people about going away. I'm suggesting she packed them herself.'

'I did it.'

'They're too neat. Even a young girl knows how to pack her things. She did that.'

He shrugged, the movement of the sling causing him pain. 'Maybe she did.'

'Maybe, or really?'

'Or-right. So she did.'

'Now we're getting somewhere. You're saying that on the night she was killed she packed her things.'

He grumbled to himself.

'Pardon? I didn't hear that.'

'I said, I suppose she must've,' he shouted.

'Then why didn't she take them with her, if she was leaving home?'

He became frantic. 'She wasna. She'd've

come back.'

George interrupted. 'I saw something once. A chap like you, in a plaster cast up to his elbow, and some not very nice people didn't like him. They hung his arm down and poured boiling water into the cast. Nasty. When they tried to get the cast off—'

'All right, George. Give him time. Why didn't she take the cases, Fletcher?'

There was terror in his eyes now. 'I dunno.'

'Did you prevent her, by force?'

'No. No, you ain't gunna say that!'

'Your kettle's boiling,' said George.

Fletcher screamed and fell across the table trying to get out. I caught him by the collar.

'Is that the truth?'

'She . . . she took 'em with her,' he cried, almost weeping, gibbering with fear.

Behind him George laughed in disbelief. The kettle made a small grating sound as he slid it off the flame, and there was a pop when he turned off the gas.

'Give me a minute, George,' I pleaded. 'If she took them, how is it they're here?'

'They was brought back.'

'Now don't come that . . .'

'They was! I tell yer, they was brought back.'

'Who by?'

'By . . .' He choked on his own spittle. 'By Reuben.'

'Reuben brought the cases back? How did *he* come by them?'

172

'He found 'em, in the road, by his gate.'

I released him. Not only was it so unlikely as to be true, but it also happened to fit. His head went down on the table, and now he was weeping in earnest.

'Don't go anywhere,' I advised him. 'There's a small matter of grievous bodily harm to answer for.'

George patted him on the head as he walked past. Fletcher's nose flattened against the table.

'I brewed your tea,' he said.

There was no question of the long way round, going back. I wanted to see Thwaites in a hurry.

'You think you've got him nailed, Dave?' said George pleasantly.

'What for?'

'Tina,' he said surprisingly. He elaborated. 'She was leaving home. Suitcase in each hand. Defenceless. He ran after her in one of his rages, and strangled her, and Reuben knew something because he found the cases.'

'You'd do anything, George, just anything, to confuse the issue over Collis's death.'

'I wasn't talking about Collis.'

'But you were. Inversely, so to speak. If Fletcher had killed Tina, he'd have had no motive to shoot Collis, so your bit about him spotting where the gun was thrown is irrelevant.'

'You don't have to sound so smug, Dave. I

just tossed it in.'

'Then toss it out again. There's the sexual assault.'

'So?'

'You're not suggesting . . .'

'I'm not suggesting anything. But he's rotten enough.'

'His own step-child? George, they'd crucify him for that, round here. These sort of people, they're a bit old-fashioned.'

He laughed, condescending to me, now. 'That sort of thing's older than fashion, Dave. Remember Oedipus?' He seemed placid.

I drove a bit faster, getting away from the idea.

The last two hundred yards was difficult. The police station was besieged, and the overflow carried into the main street.

'What the hell is it, George?'

He'd got the window down his side, and was shouting questions as I edged through. He withdrew it, his face red.

'They are old-fashioned. They don't like the police arresting Andy Partridge for exterminating Collis.'

'Oh Lord!'

I managed to get into the relative quiet of the pub yard, but even from there you could hear the rise and fall of the angry and dangerous tumult.

'You go on in if you like, George. I've got to see Thwaites.'

'Not me, mate. I'm gonna join in the fun. I don't like it, either.'

And like a great over-grown schoolboy he marched off towards the centre of it, practising as he went. 'Fascist pigs! Commie gauleiters!' No harm in embracing all his dislikes together.

'We'd better go round the back,' said Williamson from the shadows. 'We'll never get in at the front.'

'I wanted to see him.'

'He wanted to see you. Alone.'

CHAPTER TWELVE

I hadn't realised that Thwaites's office overlooked the street, but it was at once evident. Thwaites was standing a little back from the window, hands in his trousers pockets, watching the scene with interest. I felt insecure. Thwaites was relaxed.

He did not ask me to sit down.

'They're going to take this place apart, brick by brick,' I said.

'I intend to put a stop to it.'

'There's no love lost for Collis.'

'I'll go along with that.' He glanced at his watch. 'Go and look out of the window.'

I went. At the sight of my face there was a howl that made me flinch, but then they were distracted. A shout went up and became a roar, and beneath me, into the streetlight, stepped Andy Partridge.

'The mist's lifting,' I said.

'Soon see things clearer.'

I turned to face him. 'Why have you let him go?'

The tension behind me in the streets was flying away on the gusts of wild welcome.

'Because I didn't think he'd done anything.'

'There's a thousand people out there you've convinced he did.'

'Mass hysteria.'

I considered him. 'You had the footprint and the tyre print.'

'Nothing in themselves.'

'The blood on the leather coat.'

'He said he had an accident, a little while back. Somebody put his coat under his head. He and Collis have the same blood group.'

'Stretching it a bit, aren't you?'

Thwaites shrugged. 'There was also the question of the gun.'

'He could have seen where the gun was thrown into the ditch.'

He was shaking his head slowly, that half smile of his on his lips. 'The wound was made by the discharge of two barrels.'

'My partner says no.'

'Your partner, Mr. Mallin, is known to me. He was weapons expert for the Midlands, when I was a constable on the beat. But no expert could tell more at a glance than the

Medical Examiner on the table.'

'He seemed definite.'

'Coe was talking about both barrels at the same time. Close to, you get a sort of oval wound. This was round, you see, that's what put him off. Two barrels, one after the other, precisely in the same spot.'

I was silent for a moment. Then I realised I was fitting it in, seeing how that left George.

'He's quite a character,' said Thwaites.

'You mean it wasn't that gun?'

'I mean that if it was, then Andy Partridge didn't use it. Think about it. There'd be quite a bit of wangling involved . . .' He plucked at his lip. 'I remember the first time I saw him. Sergeant Coe, at that time. I was in on a job in Brum, digging out two characters who'd strangled a child they'd kidnapped. *They'd* got shotguns, now I come to recall it. Coe was the plain clothes man who'd traced them to an old warehouse. He went in alone, round the back. We waited, two dozen of us, for his signal, but all we got was one hell of an uproar, guns going off, and screams. When we got in there, one of 'em had hardly got any face left, and the other . . . they never mended his arm properly.'

'Why're you telling me this?'

'I knew he wouldn't make Inspector. Takes the law into his own hands. Lets his feelings dictate to him.'

'Which you never do?'

177

He laughed easily. 'I've trained myself. It makes life easier. But your friend . . . you realise he killed Collis, of course.'

I was aware that it had gone quiet outside. I went to the window, but there was no sign of George in the empty street. Never around when I needed him.

'You can rely on George to be unpredictable.'

'You agree it's very possible, then?'

'All I can be certain is that he wouldn't deliberately lie to me. If you're correct, then it's been one deception after the other.'

'I don't find that difficult to accept.'

'Not difficult,' I admitted, 'if you've trained yourself, as you claim to have done.'

'He's capable of it?'

'Of course. Capable of anything.'

'And clever enough?'

'Look here—what did you get me here for? If you think I'm going to fill in all your gaps, then you're going to be unlucky.'

At last he went and sat down at his desk. Still there was no paperwork in evidence.

'I don't need your help in that way,' he said at last. He shook his head. 'Unfortunately, I can put a case together from one end to the other, and tell you exactly what he did and why . . . except for one small point.'

'Now we're coming to it.'

He steepled his fingers, a habit of his. 'That meeting, Collis and his sister-in-law, was

178

carefully arranged. Secretly. Coe says he followed the woman in Collis's car. We have to accept *that*, too, because he describes it on his tape, exactly as she tells it.'

'You've played it over?'

'He leaves his car open. We have a copy. Their respective movements are confirmed up to one specific time—when he lost the BMW. Now—you get my point—for George Coe to have killed Collis he would have had to be able to get to the meeting place before she did.' He hummed to himself, considering his words. 'And she herself barely had time.'

'That's what she *said*. In the post that morning . . .'

'We've done some checking. She gets her post delivered around 7.15. The postman remembers a package that morning.'

'A package?'

'Anything larger than an ordinary letter is a package. This was ten inches by eight. She showed me the envelope. It had his official name and office address printed in the top left-hand corner. The postmark was 5.30 the previous day, the postage first class. She had destroyed the contents. You see how impossible it was for a third party to know about the site of the meeting.'

'But nevertheless, you say that George knew.'

'I say that he had to. I simply do not know how.'

I stared at him, fascinated. 'You're asking me to find that out for you?'

'You'd be doing me a favour.'

'Bring him in, why don't you, charge him, question him . . .'

He was looking at me with a slight smile, then he spread his hands expressively.

'But you're completely naïve!' I burst out. 'To imagine I'd do such a thing!'

'You know me,' he said blandly. 'You know the type. I press ahead with my career. No feelings involved, Mallin, and no regrets. I'm not going to have an unsolved murder on *my* books. Come what may. And what will come, sooner or later, is an arrest and a trial, and some poor blighter is going to get it in the neck, just to make sure my reputation doesn't suffer. You wouldn't want that—now would you. For your friend, you'll help me, because he'll only suffer if I build up a good case against somebody else.'

'Oh, cut it out.'

'Then you'll help?'

'Anybody as pitiful as you deserves a hand-out.'

'You're very understanding.'

'I'll get some truth out of him somehow. But not for you, Thwaites. For me, mate, for me.'

'I'll look forward to seeing you again, then.'

I made for the door. 'I didn't say I'd be back.'

But he held the smile, sweeping me with it

right out into the corridor.

Had I remembered to bring my pipe? Yes, I had. I knocked it out viciously on his wall, then marched away, ramming the tobacco home too tight in my agitation. Then I headed for George, where I knew he would be, the public bar of the Crown.

Reaching there was one thing, getting in was another. Being the nearest pub, naturally they had all headed there, bearing aloft, I heard later, Andy Partridge in a haze of delight. It wasn't simply a matter of being freed from arrest. He knew it, the whole blasted town knew it. The triumph was that he had killed Collis, was known to all and sundry to have killed him, and he'd got away with it.

They packed the corridors and wedged open the outside doors. The Snug was unbearable, the Smoke Room was thick, but it was in the Public that he reigned. I forced my way through, swearing, but the mood was such that I aroused laughter rather than resentment.

They had Andy on a bar stool in the centre of the bar, with a space around him. He clutched a glass dazedly, his face beaming and hot, his eyes blurred with tears. Nothing like this had ever happened to Andy. If he cleared his throat, they cheered. The din was immense, and it was *his* noise. He possessed it, and they possessed him. It was his heaven.

George was just to one side of him at the bar, in a proprietorial position, like a trainer basking in the reflected glory of his lightweight.

I said: 'George, you ought to be ashamed of yourself.'

'Give the man a bitter,' he shouted. He was obviously several ahead of me.

'How you can drink with a murderer . . .'

My words were drowned in a tumult of jeers and laughter.

'Shake his hand, Dave,' George roared. 'Go on, Andy, stick out your fist.'

'It's too sore.' He blushed, even redder than he had been.

'I suppose everybody thinks it's just bloody marvellous,' I said, looking round to challenge the opposition. 'It's all a great bit of fun. But I've just come from the Station. You listen to this, Andy my lad. Because you could well be sitting on a bundle of dynamite.'

'They let me go,' he appealed. 'They said I was free.

'For now, you young fool, for now.'

'Leave him alone,' somebody bellowed. I held up my hand.

'They've got a case against you, Andy. Make no mistake.'

'Footprints, Dave? Tyre prints? What's that?' George was suddenly more sober.

'More than that. There's the gun.'

There were cheers for that gun. Andy grinned delightedly.

'There's the fact,' I cried, raising my voice,

'that you followed the red car. Always you followed Collis, wherever he went, and if he was in a red MGB, then you followed that.'

Andy licked his lips. Then he grinned. 'Sure I followed him.'

'Then you blasted him, and went and hid in the trees because there was another car coming.'

'What's this, Dave?'

I waved George down. 'Let him have a good look at it. It ain't funny. What about it, Andy?'

He clung desperately to his triumph. 'It's what you said.'

'Then it's true? Say it out loud.'

'I blasted him, and hid in the trees.'

Another cheer. Andy was doing well.

'Then afterwards you followed *her*?'

He shook his head. There was a general inrush of breath. Out in the corridors, in the Snug and in the Smoke Room, they were silent, craning to hear. I had them now, my audience. Andy's audience. We held them with the mention of a woman.

He rallied. 'I'd gotta do that. Be sure where she went.'

'You knew where she'd go. You knew who she was. You work in the same offices.'

'All right then, I knew.'

'So why did you follow her?'

'I don't know why . . . He was dead. You've gotta . . .'

'I'm asking you because there was blood on

183

the back of your riding jacket. And the only way you'd get it was when you followed the red MGB right back to the car park at the Airport, and then, when she'd left it, you couldn't resist sliding in behind the wheel, just to see what it felt like.'

There was such a deep silence that I could hear a car's door slam a couple of streets away and the thin wailing from the café.

'He doesn't have to answer this, Dave.'

'Oh, but he does. If he wants to go on claiming the credit for killing Collis, let him justify it.'

Andy's face seemed to have shrunk. The sweat still stood on his face, like condensation on an iced cake. He wiped his mouth with the back of his hand.

'I don't . . .' he croaked, ' . . . don't have to justify shooting something like Adrian Collis.'

That drew a response. He had them again.

'To me you do. To your friends who brought you here, you do. Let's have a look at it, friend Andy. We've sketched over it so far. You followed the red car. Not the woman particularly. Not the man. Just followed whatever there was to follow.'

'It wasn't as simple as that.'

'Because it didn't mean much to you. These two people together—it wasn't significant.'

'I knew!'

'Well of course you did. You'd seen them at the office, intimate. Nothing new to you. They

184

had something going, Andy, hadn't they?'

He tried to grin. 'I guess.' His face was puckered like a monkey's, looking aged.

'You guess! You know, Andy. Collis and his sisterin-law. Oh, you knew it all right. Then can you tell me why a chap who's having it off whenever he fancies should go chasing after young women?'

'Everybody knows!'

There was a general muttering, which grew gradually as confidence was restored. 'Yeah, yeah!' they shouted.

I waited for it to die. To Andy, now, the stool was not a throne, but a torture instrument. I wouldn't release him.

'Very well. Leave that for now. Assume he was oversexed. We'll accept that you still thought he'd killed your wife, in spite of an affair you knew about.'

'He did it.'

'So you waited for your time, and your weapon. There was my friend, here, chucking a perfectly good shotgun into a ditch. You saw that, did you?'

'I saw it. Saw it all.' He gained confidence. He was licking his lips and looking round for approval. He had to have this.

'And this was the gun that you used to shoot Collis?'

'Yes, yes.' He tried to elaborate. 'Bang. Take that, you murdering bastard.'

It raised another roar.

'Just bang? Not: bang, bang?'

'Now listen, Dave, I told you—'

'And you be quiet, George. I know what I'm saying. There were two barrels of shot in Collis's chest.'

'Fired twice!' Andy cried. 'Yes, I fired twice.'

'Then you took the gun away and put it back in the ditch?'

'Well . . . I would.'

'No, you wouldn't. You'd dump it, the first chance.'

He was almost in tears of entreaty. 'But I *did*.'

'Only the trouble is, that gun was only fired once.'

They sighed and muttered. They coughed in embarrassment.

'Blast you, Dave, you're tricking him.' George clawed at my arm. I shook him off.

Andy fought for it. His eyes burned. Desperation forced the correct words out. 'I was crafty. Stuck another cartridge up one barrel.'

There was a great heave of approval at my defeat.

'And cleaned it first, Andy?'

'I'd do that. Yes.'

'When?'

'When I got home.'

'That was very clever thinking. You present a good case. Sergeant Williamson is making notes, over there by the door.'

That was a slight error, nearly leading to the early demise of Williamson, but Andy rescued him. He laughed. Out of that haggard face it was hideous, but he laughed and said: 'Let him. They can't prove it.'

And half a dozen men actually slapped Williamson on the back, because he couldn't prove it, and had, in fact, only been looking amused.

'As long as there's no proof, that makes it fine, I suppose.' He nodded, wary, trembling. 'Because you're convinced that Collis killed those three girls?'

'The same as everybody else.'

'Not the same as everybody else, Andy. What about the suitcases?'

Behind me, George growled. He'd seen what I was getting at.

'What suitcases?' Andy asked weakly. There was a general sigh.

'Tina's cases, Andy. Reuben knew about them, because it was he who took them back to her house. Reuben knew, and he's in hospital now.'

'I didn't know about any cases.'

'Come on now. Reuben was trying to tell us. He tried to tell Mrs. Collis, because it was so important to her. Tina was leaving home. She'd have told your wife. You must have known.'

Andy was baffled. 'Yes, I knew. But not,' he

187

added quickly, 'about the cases.'

'Are you telling me that Reuben didn't tell *you*. Almost his next door neighbour. Intimately involved. We can ask him . . .'

'He said he took 'em back to the house.'

'So she did actually leave?'

'Yes, yes. Let me alone.'

'And left her cases on the road?'

'I suppose.'

'You know! Reuben told you. He found them there. And why should she leave them there unless she got a lift? Why leave them *if* she got a lift?'

'Tossed 'em out,' he shouted hoarsely.

'And you really thought that, Andy? You knew her. You'd know that all she ever owned was probably in those cases, and yet you'd accept that she tossed them out of the car? Never. You're a bright lad. You'd see that was not true. And you'd tell yourself that somehow it didn't fit Collis, either. He knew her too. Why should he alarm her? So you'd be doubtful. What's happened since to change your mind?'

He stared at me, sweat trickling from his chin, his eyes hollow. 'He did it,' he croaked.

'But you didn't believe that!' I shouted at him. 'It was the cases that made you doubt it. Damn it all, even Reuben thought it was strange. Strange enough, anyway, to want to tell it to Mrs. Collis. Christ, man, were you all terrified of Jonas Fletcher?'

'It wasn't . . . not that . . .' But he was too near to breakdown.

The silence now took on a different texture. An idol falls further than its original base.

'I'm sick of this,' I said. 'You and your games. You'd got no motive at all for killing Collis, and the only weapon you could've used wasn't the one.' For the first time I took a drink of my beer. It was flat. It matched my mood.

Andy sagged on the stool.

'So tell me, Andy, why Jonas Fletcher had to terrify you all, just because Tina left home. Tell me what frightened *him*.'

And Andy, released now from his pose, knowing his guilt had melted away, poured it out with compressed anger.

'Because she wasn't sixteen, she was fifteen, and there'd be trouble, and the police askin', if they knew she'd actually left home. Sweet Jesus! The bastard, the dirty, stinking bastard! She told my wife. He wouldn't let her alone. She couldn't sleep and didn't dare rest. He was after her, and he'd . . . he'd . . .' He covered his face with his hands.

We had it. For that, Jonas Fletcher had so terrified the other two that none of them had come forward with a minor point in Collis's favour. It might not have saved him, but it would have helped.

I would have said that it was impossible for such a throng to melt away without a sound.

189

And yet, when I looked round, there was nobody there. Andy sat in the shadow of his triumph, and I had taken it away from him. It was very much later when I realised what I had really taken.

'Get off home, son,' said George wearily, and it was I who'd done all the work.

Andy stirred. George put a hand to his arm. We watched him move out of the door. He seemed afraid to face the night.

'That was good,' said George. 'You're surpassing yourself tonight. I hope you had a good reason.'

'Good enough. I wanted to prove he couldn't have killed Collis.'

He snorted in disgust. 'Fancy ideas about the shotgun! I could take it to pieces, argument by . . .'

'I'm sure you could.'

'And that bit about the suitcases! I could give you several reasons why Collis'd dump 'em there, even possibly on the way back.'

'You could, George. A psychiatrist could. But not Andy. To Andy it was a valid point.'

'It didn't convince me.'

'It didn't have to. You didn't know about them until tonight.'

'So now we're coming to it.'

'And if you had—as you've just said—it wouldn't convince you of Collis's innocence.'

'You chopped him to pieces—for *me?* I should be grateful.'

'But you won't be, I'm sure. Thwaites has got it all lined up, and he's only one breath away from charging you. But it suited you fine to have Andy around, as good as a confessed murderer, because you knew he was safe. So I had to wipe him off the slate, and all we've got is a nice polished surface, with your fat face reflected in it. Oh yes, you can laugh. You're there, mate, you and your motive, your means, and your opportunity.'

'It's interesting, I'll give you that.'

'You did not throw the gun away. You kept it in the back of your car until after the murder. You'd found out about the affair, George, and deliberately used it. You followed *her,* knowing who you were following, and you let her drop you at a convenient point for you to be able to get to the log house first. Before even Collis got there. Then you went and dumped the gun in the ditch, and phoned from a box close to there, before heading back to Filsby. You'd be capable of working things out like that.'

'Under your nose, Dave? I'd be taking a big risk, with you so damned smart.'

'Or you were a bit too clever. The gun was too subtle, that's what really gets me. You didn't flatter me much, assuming I'd miss the point about the gun.'

'It doesn't help, making me feel stupid. What point about the gun?'

'The two barrels being discharged . . . and

191

it's no good arguing about it. The Medical Examiner says it was so, both barrels fired at Collis. It looked like one, superficially, because it was one after the other, in the same spot. Now, that could have happened normally, by accident, but only you, George, in a radius of fifty miles, would know that the Medical Examiner could prove two barrels were fired with only one entry wound. And only you could know how to take advantage of that.'

You can say this for George, he was treating this with serious consideration, his eyes calm, his voice level.

'I get your point.'

'You could have fired two barrels from Fletcher's gun, carefully into Collis's chest, clean it up, re-load, and fire one again into the air. *Then* ditch the gun, knowing you could produce it as the possible murder weapon. And knowing—and this is the point—that the police would later say that this gun, the one associated with you, could not be the murder weapon because it had only been fired once.'

'But there must be a snag, because I haven't been arrested. A breath away, you said.'

'One point. Thwaites wanted me to find out how the devil you knew where to go, when it was a secret meeting. And you'd need to know, to get there first.'

'And you'd really expect me to tell you that?'

'About as much as Thwaites expected me to

192

go back and pass it on.'

He finished my stale beer in one long gulp.

'Well, that's all right then.'

CHAPTER THIRTEEN

I prowled our room, waiting for George. He had said he wanted to make a phone call. I waited, wondering how the hell I was going to knock it into his head. I had shown him—hell, I'd scrubbed my brain to the bone, working it out—I'd shown him that he was out there on his own as a suspect. But had he been impressed? Like hell he had!

The door opened. I turned to face him, angry arguments at the ready. But when I saw his face I said nothing.

His chin was down and his eyes were angry. 'I phoned the hospital.'

'Reuben?'

'He died a few minutes ago.'

I felt sick. 'I'm sorry.'

'You coming, Dave, or do I do it on my own?'

I knew what he intended. 'There's things we should discuss.'

'Please yourself. Discuss 'em in the car. We'll take mine.'

I held out my hand. 'Give me your keys, George.'

He stared at me.

'You're a rotten driver at the best of times.'

'I'll drive,' he growled, and that was that.

He took the Renault out of the pub's car park in a spray of ashes. I managed to refrain from comment. He headed out of town.

'You're not stupid, George. You can't help but see the sort of case they've got against you.'

A patrol car in a lay-by flicked his heads in protest at our speed, but did not follow us.

'You made your point.'

'Then for heaven's sake let's do some thinking about it. If there's one point you've missed, and Thwaites gets a sniff of it, one detail that'd show how you could've known where the meeting was to be, then you'd be nailed.'

'Fletcher first.' I caught the gleam of his teeth in the dashlights. 'Then what? If we find this detail, what do we do then, Dave?'

'We destroy it.'

He took it fast, once we were out of the mist. The moon was down. The night sky was heavy again with the snow. The underside of the clouds reflected a glow.

'What sort of detail? he asked, juggling with the gears. 'What am I supposed to have missed? Or what am I supposed to have seen, and the rest of you've missed?'

'Keep your mind on the road.'

'The letter Amanda Greaves received?' he

persisted. 'Am I supposed to have got a sight of that?'

'Impossible. It wasn't so much a letter as a package. Ten by eight. That strike a note, does it?'

'Nothing.'

'What's the rush?' He had just taken a forty corner at sixty. 'You worried about something?'

'That glow in the sky.'

I had thought at first that it was the reflection of a large town's street lamps, but there was only the Chase out there. Nowhere closer than Lichfield. It grew and then subsided. Grew again. George's fist was now almost permanently on the horn. He threw the Renault into those long, sweeping, rising bends.

'It's up on the top,' I said.

There was no doubt, now, that there was a fire. A forest fire at that time of the year was unlikely, and I knew of only one building up there. We charged past Goldwater's place, the light dimly detectable half way up the long farm drive, screamed past Fletcher's, his light on too, and on past Andy Partridge's, which was dark. I did not recognise the spot where the gun had been ditched.

'It's Firbelow!' I shouted.

The engine took on a deep, throaty roar as the car went into the steeper part of the climb. The red glow was separated from the clouds now, reaching for them in broken tongues of flame. As we came round the last bend, the blazing house was fully visible.

That roof would go first, cedar shingles and tar-felt. The fact that the flames reached out through the roof did not mean that the whole building was lost. But through the front windows the blaze was rioting in every room, and the hall was an inferno. The gate was still open. George drove through it without even easing speed, and I felt the jolt as the swinging tail touched the gate post.

Delia Collis was screaming on the front lawn. She was not aware of us. As we skidded to a halt behind her, she flung herself once more—her clothes were smoking—into the hall. But the heat threw her back. George caught her in his arms. He clutched her tightly to him because he might suppress the smouldering.

From inside the house, somewhere at the back, came the frantic baying of Major.

'Round the back,' I shouted, and we ran, George a foot or two behind me.

The curtains along the run of the wide windows were drawn, but even as I watched I saw flames flickering at their hems.

George said: 'Gimme your coat, Dave.'

My poor old motoring coat! He flung it over his head. He could not have seen anything, but all he wanted to go was straight. You're not supposed to let air into a burning room.

George took in a complete set of double-glazing and ten feet of heavy curtain, but the flames that welcomed the air were neutralised when the complete bundle of George, coat and curtain rolled over on them. Tumbling, he disappeared into the black smoke, before the room burst with a sudden flush of new flame.

He'd left me no cover, even had my coat. I bellowed: 'George!' But the roar of the flames took it away. My throat was hot when I drew in breath, and ashes rained on me.

'George!'

I plunged at the destroyed window, and Major chose the same moment to leap free. We are much the same weight, but he was moving faster. I had a brief impression of a huge grey shape with glaring eyes and terrible teeth, with the hunched grey jockey of the cat clinging to his back, and then he'd rolled me over and was bounding free.

'You all right, Dave?'

George picked me up and dusted me off. He had no eyebrows, and there was no sign of my motoring coat.

'How long've you been lying there? he asked.

My head ached. 'The dog and the cat got out. We'd better tell Delia.'

'In a second.' He drew his hand over his face. 'They were in the kitchen. The fire started in the workroom.' He seemed to be picking his words carefully and painfully. 'I

197

could smell the petrol. It never goes away. Petrol in the workroom, Dave. It got me thinking. That morning Collis died, I went in there. I've got a mental image . . . one of his picture frames was empty.'

'A ten by eight?'

'His drawing of the log house. Dave, he couldn't have been playing cloak and dagger with Amanda, surely. You tell me he wasn't. Tell me he didn't send her that drawing to say where he'd meet her.'

He had reason to be exhausted, but he was too beaten for the fire to explain it all. Sometimes you have to treat George like a frightened child, and encourage him.

'I'm afraid that's what it means.'

'And Delia saw it was missing, too?'

'I'm sorry, George, but it's the only explanation.'

He turned and looked at the blazing house, close to total destruction now. He spoke with wonder in his voice. 'She did that, just to hide the fact? Just because she couldn't put the drawing back.'

'Let's go and ask her, George.'

He dragged himself into action, and I followed him round to the front. We could hear the fire engines fighting their way up the rise.

She was lying moaning on the lawn, Major panting beside her. At first he wouldn't let us touch her, but I saw the cat and gave him to

Major to play with. Major nuzzled him. Delia was bad, having been wearing artificial fibres. On her legs, parts of the slacks were embedded blackly into the flesh. George knelt and lifted her head.

Men ran past us. An officer stopped and shouted was there anybody inside, and I said no but we'd need an ambulance.

'My beautiful home!' she whispered.

'It wouldn't have been the same,' said George softly. I glanced down at him. His eyes looked naked. 'Not without Adrian. Your home, your husband . . .'

She smiled weakly. Her eyes were black, her hair singed. 'My marriage,' she agreed softly.

It had been like a package to her, one that came all wrapped neatly at the altar. All she had had to do was cut the string.

She coughed, gently at first, then rackingly. George waited for it to cease.

'Nothing was going to break it up, was it? The more the difficulties, the more you dug in your heels. Not even a rape. Not a murder. Not three. You could put that behind you, because Adrian was yours.'

'Together . . .' she protested. 'Both of us together. We could have done anything.' Her voice was harsh.

But George was reaching for her motivation. 'You'd hate him for the murders. That was a threat to your beautiful marriage, and it was *his* doing.'

'No, no!'

'The ambulance is here, George.'

'All right,' he snapped. 'Delia—didn't you care? Didn't you feel anything against him for those killings?'

'He couldn't help himself. Dear Adrian. I could have given him anything. I tried. He never blamed me when I couldn't give him that. Not truly. I tried. Believe me, I tried.'

'George! You've only got a minute.'

'Delia,' he said softly, bending close, 'we know you tried. It didn't change a thing. To Adrian you were precious, and not to be hurt. He cherished you.'

Her eyes narrowed. The blistered lips tightened with pain and distress. 'Then why did he go to Amanda? He should have come to me. I would have comforted him and calmed him and protected him. But he went to Amanda.'

'After all three?'

'He should have come to me!' she tried to scream, but it came out as a shrill whisper. 'Me, to cry to. Me . . . to appeal to. Not to her. Not that bitch.'

'So you'd never understood why he hadn't seemed distressed after the three murders. It'd worried you and disturbed you. You'd have preferred him to come crying on your breast. But then you found out about the affair. Is that it?'

'I hated him, then.'

'And you saw the significance of the missing drawing?'

'Excuse me, sir. If you'll just stand clear.'

George glanced up impatiently. 'A second. The drawing,' he repeated. 'You saw the meaning, and realised where they were going to meet. You went there and waited, with Adrian's gun. And there, because he had not come to you in his troubles, you shot him.'

'Didn't he deserve that?'

'I don't know. We should have guessed earlier, then we might have saved your home. We could have saved you burning it to hide the fact that the drawing was missing.'

'I wanted . . . to burn . . . his workroom. Only that.'

I should have realised. Andy Partridge . . . such a straightforward chap. He'd found out about the affair, and naturally he'd do just one thing. He'd tell Delia.

'Really, sir, you must move. The lady needs attention.' The man sounded shocked at George's lack of feeling.

George got to his feet. He grasped my elbow, but couldn't find the words. I helped him.

'They'd never sentence her, George. They'll let you give evidence. Don't worry. I blame myself. I should've realised that Andy would tell her about the affair—and it's knowing about it that's driven her to kill him.'

They picked up the stretcher. Delia made a

small protest, and they paused. Only her face was visible, now, the burns growing into fierce red blotches. She had heard what I said, and gestured weakly to me. I bent my head close to her.

'So stupid . . . stupid of you. Of course Andy didn't tell me. She did. Phoned that morning. Said I'd never see him alive again.' Her smile was suddenly grimly angelic. 'But I did.'

We watched the ambulance drive away. George stood stolidly beside me.

He spoke wearily. 'Did you know, Dave?'

I wiped my sweating face, and the handkerchief came up black. 'No more than a feeling on the motivation side of it. I reckoned she'd forgive Adrian anything except his going to Amanda after killing those three girls. Never that. But I couldn't see how she'd found out about the affair, unless Andy had told her. But he didn't give one hint of that. And I couldn't see any way at all that she'd know where to go.'

I couldn't put into words the fact that it had been my suspicion of George which had come between us and an earlier realisation of the truth. But I could see from George's eyes that he saw what I was thinking.

'Think about something else,' he said quietly. 'How about deciding what we're going to do with one Great Dane and one grey cat.'

We considered them. They sat mournfully beside us, apparently aware of the precariousness of their position. We looked at each other.

'Amanda?' I suggested.

'Why not?' But he wasn't giving it all his thought. 'Fletcher . . .'

Not while he was in such a murderous mood. 'Not now, George. Let's get rid of the animals first.'

The flaring light reddened his face. He straightened his shoulders and looked beyond me at the frantic activity. 'Animals first,' he grunted.

Major was no trouble. He got in the back at the first invitation. Smoke was more reluctant. I don't suppose he fancied being stuck in there with a big dog. We persuaded him. We chased him and caught him—when he was good and ready—and heaved him in. He stuck five claws in Major's nose, just to establish who was boss.

It was very late when we reached the flat. The fog on the motorway was bad; it heads for motorways. There were no lights on in Flat 27. We rang a number of times, and Amanda was not in a good mood when she opened up.

'We wanted to ask you a favour,' I said, and we marched right in.

She was wearing a heavy dressing gown over pyjamas. She saw me looking at it, and laughed, slightly apologetically.

'Adrian's. All I've got left of him. What was the favour? And please be quick—you woke me up.'

Yet the dark chestnut hair was perfect. 'Two favours, really. The first is to tell us why you lied when we saw you before.'

'If you're going to be offensive . . .'

'Not at all. I was perfectly polite. Let me explain something. Your sister is in hospital with severe burns. When she's fit enough, she'll be charged with the murder of her husband.'

She eyed me levelly. Only by a small grimace did she display any emotion.

'It seems to me that you're proving I told you the truth. I said I found him dead in the MGB. I did. I had to put him in his own car.'

'That wasn't what I meant. You told us that he came to you from three rape-murders. That you comforted him and tidied him. *That* was a lie.'

Now the mouth was expressing emotion— contempt. 'You suggested it yourself. I merely went along with it.'

'I hadn't got all the evidence then. I didn't know that Tina's suitcases were found less than half a mile from her home.'

'And?' She raised her eyebrows challengingly.

'We've had some talk about what it means, Miss Greaves. I've already used the fact to show that it makes the question of Collis's guilt doubtful. But I'm not going to bore you with that, because it shows something else much more interesting—to you, anyway. You see, it is quite unacceptable that Collis would

204

offer a lift to a young girl he knew—a reasonable enough action under the circumstances—and immediately throw out her cases. It would alarm her. It would be stupid and gain nothing for him. So, assuming it *was* Collis, we'd have to accept that he threw them out later.'

George prowled. He paused and glanced at me, and then smiled.

'What's this getting to?' Amanda demanded.

'I'm wondering when, exactly, later. Imagine it. The cases on his rear seat, say. The obvious place to dump them was at Filsby, with her body. But say he forgot. Say he was simply driving home, and then remembered . . . well, he might toss them out then, and by coincidence near her own home. But he wasn't driving home, was he? He was coming here. And here is around thirty miles from Filsby. Thirty miles, in which to remember and dump them. Then there's a period here, also in which he might remember, and work out where to unload them. Twenty-five miles back home, during any of which he could have successfully disposed of them. But they were found near her home! I'm saying, Miss Greaves, that those cases might not have any great relevance as to Collis's guilt, but by heaven they show that if he *was* guilty, he certainly didn't bring his guilt here.'

'You must enjoy listening to yourself.'

'Do you deny it?'

'Deny what?' she snapped. 'That he came here—or that he was guilty?'

'Both,' I challenged.

But she was considering my intensity with tolerant amusement. It was wasted on her. Then she moved a hand negligently.

'Of course he didn't kill them.'

I was a little rattled. 'Then you'll be amused to hear why your sister killed Adrian. It was simply because of that, because she believed he'd murdered them, and then had run to you with their deaths on his hands. When he should have gone to her.'

'Delia was always a fool.'

I have often marvelled at the intensity of hatred that can exist between two sisters. George was looking as though he was sucking something sour. He didn't want to speak to her.

'But not you. You're no fool,' I said. 'A very clever woman like you, you'd detect that. You'd understand her worry and puzzlement, and you'd prod at it with implications, driving her mad. But she didn't *know*. She didn't even know of the affair with you, until you phoned her up that morning. You couldn't resist that. There was going to be an end to all the farce. You told her she wouldn't see him again alive. You intended to kill him.'

'Really, this is quite absurd.'

'Why trouble to deny it? You're not going

to be tried for anything. At least, nothing to do with the murder. Perhaps something in the past, though.'

'I don't see why I should listen to this.'

'You were quick enough to seize on it when I suggested he'd come to you with murder on his hands. It sketched you in as a romantic figure—sympathetic. That mattered to you, I'd suggest, if your real motives were unpleasant, and even degrading. I'm guessing here, I admit, but I think I could persuade a police fraud squad to look into it. I wonder what they'd find if they look back at the County Council contracts that Adrian Collis acquired, and who wangled them for him. And then, what a splendid hold you had over him. You stood to lose your job, perhaps be prosecuted for corruption, but *he* stood to lose everything, his career, the lot.'

'I loved him,' she cried. 'He loved me.'

'I think not.' I was very tired and my head was singing. I concentrated. 'Delia said there was one thing she couldn't give him. Something you could—his sex life. Give him, and demand from him. I get the feeling that it palled for him, but you'd got both, then, to command him with, your sex and your hold over him. You called the tune. You said when and where, and he'd come running, half fascinated, half afraid.'

'Damn you, I'm not listening to this.'

'Oh, but you are. If my friend has to hold

you down, you'll listen. And how did it end, Amanda? Did you have a flaming row and he told you to go to hell?'

'Who told you this?' she screamed.

'And did you, perhaps, get your own back by phoning the police and putting them on to Adrian as a possible sex murderer? That's a bit wild, even for you, my dear. You couldn't have done that.'

She laughed wildly. 'Oh, couldn't I!'

'No wonder he didn't want you to give evidence. A fine alibi you'd build for him! But I forget, you build a good alibi. That was yours, the day he died, your whole, detailed design. He refused to meet you again, but you'd threaten and cajole and plead, and in the end he'd agree, just for a bit of peace. But he'd got two lumbering private eyes watching him. Tell him how to get away from them, and he'd see you one last time. So you told him. It was going to be his last time, right enough. You intended to kill him.'

'With that thing!' she cried hysterically. 'You said yourself . . .'

I shook my head. 'The one you showed us, Amanda? No. But what you produced was one of a presentation pair. I expect the other's quite serviceable.'

I stood and waited. George did not move. She challenged me with her eyes, and she knew I was laughing at her. She couldn't stand that. With a sudden bound she pounced on the same drawer. We did not move. She turned, waving the gun.

George laughed. 'Poor Adrian. He didn't stand much chance, caught between two fighting sisters.' It had been a nerve-tingling, painful laugh.

'We'd better go,' I said.

'You're not leaving here,' she shouted.

I put my hand on the door. 'The second favour,' George remembered.

'Oh yes. Delia's dog, and her cat. We thought you'd look after them for her.'

'You must be insane!'

'Perhaps you're right. You could be in custody, yourself, very soon. Good night.'

We left. I closed the door behind us. The shot from inside seemed a great distance away, and I heard the bullet strike the door panel. It did not penetrate.

'Fletcher,' said George, who never gives up.

'Let me drive, George. I just want to make one apology on the way. And then we can go home.'

After a few miles I said:

'Collis expected it, George. He was trying to shake free of Amanda, but she forced the meeting. He expected trouble, and when he took me up there it was to clue me in—just in case.'

But George was still sore at his misjudgement of Collis.

'You don't let anything drop, do you! I

209

suppose now you're thinking about who killed the girls, if he didn't.'

'The police will be.'

He grunted. 'And I bet you won't let that drop.'

'Not very far, George, I'll promise you that.'

He was silent, thinking that one out.

Major sat on the seat behind him. From time to time he licked George's neck.

'Get a move on,' he said.

Andy was just wheeling his bike out of the gate as we approached. I swerved in, cutting him off, and got out. He looked startled. There were two suitcases strapped on behind.

'You'll never get your leg over that lot,' I told him.

'I'll manage.'

'Going away? No need to leave the district, you know, just because I proved you couldn't have killed Collis.'

He was confused. The crash hat hung over his handlebars.

'I can't stay here.' The fear in his eyes might have been from a memory of how I'd treated him before. 'What did you want?'

'To apologise.'

He frowned. 'I'd better be going.'

'No. please. Hear me out. Back there, in the pub, I pulled out a few stops. It happened to be very important to me to remove you from the list of suspects for Collis's death. I'm sorry, Andy. I knew I was hurting you, snatching that triumph away. But I didn't realise how important it was to you in another way. I see now. If everybody accepted that you'd killed Collis, it'd have to be because you thought he'd killed your wife. Revenge. Just that. I see now that you were desperately trying to hide the fact that you knew damn well he hadn't.'

He wasn't saying anything. I went on: 'It's why I want to apologise. I really didn't know I was robbing you of so much. It was stupid of me, missing the meaning of Tina's cases. She was leaving home. You might even have known it. She'd accept a lift from you, but how could you carry the girl *and* the cases? You'd put 'em on your tank, Andy, but it wouldn't do, and you'd toss 'em away. And if Tina protested, what good would that do her on a bike? She couldn't jump off if you were going fast, not until you stopped, and that'd be too late for her. They're the quiet ones, Andy, the genuine sex maniacs. They go from one extreme to the other. Poor Madge Goldwater was the first, and then little Tina, coming to your house, and ignoring you. That would've been the worst thing she could do.'

His eyes were quite blank in the reflected lights from the heads. Calmly he put on his crash hat, a full-face one, locking himself away from me. Into his own tunnel.

'Reuben knew,' I said, refusing to raise my voice. 'I suspect that Jonas Fletcher knew, but they were both trapped in Fletcher's fear that

211

he'd be exposed himself. So Jonas watched your home from his window, and Reuben told your wife. I've no doubt that he did. He was a teller, that one. And Marilyn was on her way to the phone that night. She'd told you where she was going—to phone the police, not her mother. She'd probably told you while you were making love. It'd seem a good time.'

He protested. That last taunt drew a muffled bleat of protest.

I relented. 'Or perhaps she was only sad, that you could be so gentle with her, and not with the others, Andy.'

This time I'd struck home. He was sobbing inside his private helmet, steaming it, but unable even to see the steam. He struggled with the bike.

'There's no point,' I said, but he got his leg over and kicked it off.

I'd assumed he could never get through; the car's nose was far into the ditch. But he tried. He flicked into first and raced the engine, then shot off, pitching and kicking, and suddenly was clear.

That was when I wished we had the Porsche. I sprang in behind the wheel, but I couldn't swing out the car's nose quickly enough. The rear light was disappearing. I spun the wheels and turned after him, racing up into third.

'You could've asked me to hold him,' said George.

I didn't reply. Our heads picked him up. We

were near to sixty down the rise towards Fletcher's.

Perhaps Jonas had noticed activity up at Andy's, from his position at the window. I tell myself he believed that at last Andy was on his way to the police with the full story. Anyway, there he was, his cast a flash of white, suddenly in Andy's headlight. I don't think Andy even saw him. At the last second there was a slight wobble, and Jonas tried to jump clear. The skidding bike caught him, and Jonas tumbled across the road. The bike upended and went skidding on.

A crash hat saves you head injuries. Head on to a gatepost, you break your neck. One glance at Andy was enough. I turned to Jonas.

His face was mashed, his body twisted in a nasty way, and barely managing those rasping, raking breaths a man takes when his ribs have been broken in and they're as near as damnit piercing his lungs.

'Get to the phone, George.'

'Yes.'

'Oh, and leave me your coat.'

'He's not having *my* coat.'

I spread my jacket over him. By the time I got it back, I was near frozen.

George said: 'We seem to spend a lot of time watching ambulances drive away, Dave. It was the same one as collected Reuben.'

'Remarkable. Let's go home.'

The trouble was that we were still lumbered

with Major and Smoke, about all we had gained from that case. I wondered if I could get them in the Porsche.

'You're not taking them back to Elsa, Dave, surely.' George laughed. 'She'll chuck you all out.'

'She'll love Major. Damn it, George, she even likes you. And he's much more friendly.'

And so it was. Smoke, at the time of writing, has not been eaten.

We hope you have enjoyed this Large Print book. Other Chivers Press or Thorndike Press Large Print books are available at your library or directly from the publishers.

For more information about current and forthcoming titles, please call or write, without obligation, to:

Chivers Press Limited
Windsor Bridge Road
Bath BA2 3AX
England
Tel. (01225) 335336

OR

G.K. Hall & Co.
295 Kennedy Memorial Drive
Waterville
Maine 04901
USA

All our Large Print titles are designed for easy reading, and all our books are made to last.

96